RECKLESS
Love

KENDALL RYAN
New York Times and USA Today
BESTSELLING AUTHOR

Editing by Pam Berehulke, Bulletproof Editing

Cover Design by Helen Williams, All Booked Out

Formatting by Liz Hellebuyck

ISBN-13: 978-1505319729
ISBN-10: 1505319722

About the Book

One reckless fighter.

One night of passion she can't forget.

The battle for sex and love is fierce and unrelenting.

And love is about to knock him on his ass.

Reckless Love can be read as a standalone novel, but is a follow up to the *New York Times* and *USA Today* bestseller *Hard to Love*.

One

The worst part about training mode was the no-pussy rule.

My intense training schedule, brutal workouts, and strict diet were nothing compared to the hell of not being able to satisfy my needy cock. I had a fight in less than a week, which meant I wasn't going to see any action anytime soon, and the beautiful girl bouncing before me pushed every button I had. Pornographic thoughts ripped through my brain, making it difficult to concentrate on anything but the pulse throbbing in my erection.

A one-way mirror in the office faced the gym's solitary treadmill. I'd come in to grab a drink from the mini fridge and was in the office when MacKenzie arrived, so when she jumped on the treadmill for her morning run, I figured I might as well sit for a minute and take in the view. But it was such a fucking cocktease, I wanted to punch someone.

Her body was a twelve out of ten. My dick was telling me to pull her hot ass off the treadmill, take her in the shower, spread her legs, and give her the best fuck she'd ever had.

MacKenzie was a treat for all the senses. From the breathy gasps of exertion pushing past her parted lips, to the rhythmic way her tits bounced, and the delectable feminine scent of deodorant and sweat I could smell whenever I was stupid enough to wander near her.

Though it wasn't just about her fantastic tits and perfect ass. She had those in spades, but there was more to her. I could see it in her now. When most people went for a run, their faces relaxed and their eyes became unfocused as they zoned out. Their body might be running, but their mind was somewhere else as they bobbed along to their music.

When Kenzie ran, it wasn't just her body in motion. Behind her gentle expression was a sense of determination. Initially I thought she was running away from something, but there was no fear in her eyes, only clarity of purpose. No, she wasn't running from anything, she was running toward something.

Strength and determination in a woman were sexy as hell. I added those attributes to the list of things I liked about this girl, as if there weren't enough already. I loved watching her push forward. Her confidence and her zing, combined with her...

Well, combined with her amazing tits. Perky and palm-sized, they were perfect. I couldn't stop watching them bounce as she ran, the same way they would bounce if she rode me. Who invented one-way mirrors? I could fucking kiss them.

But I'd had my chance with her, and I screwed it up. Now she wouldn't give me the time of day.

So this was all I could do—sit and watch from afar. Or nearby, now that she worked at the gym I trained in every single day. I should have switched gyms when she started working here, but all my fights were set up through the owner, Chris. Besides, Chris had worked hard to get me where I was today. Leaving him now that I was finally on the verge of breaking through would be a dick move.

So I was stuck. Who could dream up a more frustrating hell?

MacKenzie

My morning run was always better if I had a good view from the treadmill. The free weights were set up right next to my machine, and since I was at a mostly male gym that focused on mixed martial arts fighting, my odds for having a great run were excellent.

Today, however, the view was rather dismal. There were only a few guys lifting weights, and they were featherweights. I hated to use the word scrawny with any of these guys, because they all had serious muscle, but compared to the other guys at the gym, they were a bit…smallish.

Since there was nothing good to look at while I ran, I zoned out. I couldn't help it. At only nine in the morning, a girl was allowed to mentally check out for a moment or two. So I was startled when Ian came out of the office just a few feet from me. Almost fell off the dang machine.

The one-way mirror in the office looked right out onto the treadmill. How long had he been back there? Not that he would have seen anything he liked. *The prick.*

Our eyes met for a second. His square jaw clenched and his cool blue gaze darted away from mine. He rubbed the back of his neck with his hand. The small motion emphasized the bulging arm muscles that came out of his shirtsleeve. I swallowed and caught myself licking my lips. I hated that my body still wanted him, that *I* still wanted him.

He paused for a moment next to the treadmill and chewed his lip as if he was considering saying hello.

Keep walking, asshat.

As if he'd heard my thoughts, he started moving again up to the front of the gym.

Cade was here. I waved across the room to him. Every Saturday morning, Cade came to spar with Ian. It was cute how they worked at their little bromance, even though Cade and Alexa were practically married and spent all their time together.

I saw Alexa every Thursday on our regular girls' night, but that was often the only time I'd see her now that we no longer worked together at the hospital. I sometimes worried that all it would take was Cade popping the question for her to be pulled away from me altogether. I was used to saying good-bye to people, but Alexa had been around so long, she was like family. The only family I'd ever had, really. Growing up in foster homes, I'd never had anyone who was a *forever* person, but Alexa was close, the closest I'd come.

Um, and not in that way, either. I was into guys. And speaking of guys, my view had just improved exponentially.

Ian was in the practice cage with Cade, and they both had their shirts off. *Mmm.* Cade—Mr. Former Porn Star—had a nice chest. I could see why they paid him to take it all off, but he wasn't really my type. He was such a nice guy. Who would have thought the adult-film star who could pull off a four-hour erection would be such a sweetie? Also, Alexa would kick my ass just for appreciating his nice pecs. Or she'd try, anyway.

Ian, on the other hand, I could hardly put into words. He trained here at the gym six hours a day, six days a week, and had the body to prove it. His arms were rock hard, and his shoulder and back muscles were defined and firm. I wanted to trace my fingers along them and tickle his skin. And his abs—

Oops. I almost fell off the treadmill trying to see his abs. Anyway, his abs were flipping solid. I didn't know why they call them a six-pack since he clearly had eight well-defined muscles there, and I would love to run my tongue over each and every one of them.

Don't even get me started with his eyes. Cool blue, and always so serious and business-like, but deep. Sometimes I thought back to that night, the way he looked at me as if he was going to take care of me. As if he'd never let anyone hurt me.

It was so easy to fall into his gaze that night and lose myself. It made me wish I could get wrapped up in him again.

But I never would. Not after that night.

Two

IAN

I was having a hard time not killing Cade. It was easier blocking his hits than it was keeping him uninjured. "Take out your tampon and fight, you pussy," I taunted.

Now that he'd pretty much given up fighting, I could wipe the floor with him blindfolded with both hands tied behind my back. But the guy was like a brother to me, so I took it easy on him. Or at least, I tried not to send him to the ER.

Cade threw himself at me harder. "I have documented proof that I'm no pussy. I know you've seen my videos. It's all there. All ten inches of lady-loving meat," he spat, hitting back at me verbally.

What a douche-rocket. He might be my best friend, but there was no way in hell I'd ever watch one of his old porn videos. I shuddered at the thought.

He almost got a hit in. It was hard to pay attention when MacKenzie was running on that damn treadmill. It was impossible to look away when she ran in those tight, ass-hugging shorts and that tank top—the kind with a built-in bra that hardly supported her beautiful tits as she bounced along.

I tugged at my own baggy shorts. *Down, boy.*

I knew it would be stupid to hire MacKenzie on as the gym medic. She was a distraction. But when I'd heard she was laid off from the hospital, I couldn't stand the idea of her being without a job, so I'd talked Chris into hiring her. Not that she knew anything about my involvement with her employment here. It was better that she not know.

But I wasn't the only one distracted by her. The minute she started, there was a spike in fight-related injuries. I didn't know if her hot ass was distracting the guys, or if they'd deliberately ramped up their machismo to gain her attention—and got themselves hurt in the process. Hell, I wouldn't have been surprised if the little shits were faking injury just to steal some one-on-one time with her.

Cade socked me in the gut.

"*Oof.*" I fought for breath and clutched my abdomen, which smarted like a bitch. And *that* was why you had to remain focused in the cage.

I turned my attention back to Cade, who was dancing around like a little boy, damn proud of himself for that last hit. Good for him. "You hit like a five-year-old," I told him, but he could tell I was still trying to catch my breath.

Cade smirked at me. "Maybe if you stopped thinking about your dick and got into the fight, you wouldn't be losing to a hobby fighter right now."

Oh, it's on.

I bounced around him as I got my breathing under control, then charged him, picked him up into a fireman's hold, and took us both down to the mat. Still careful to not kill the poor guy. I easily pulled him into a hold and applied pressure.

"Who's a pussy?" I asked.

He twisted around. "You are," he grumbled with a smile.

I applied more pressure. "Who's a pussy?"

His face turned red, but he held out a few more beats before he couldn't stand it anymore. "I am," he grunted through clenched teeth.

"Good boy."

I released him and helped him back up on his feet. As we resumed sparring, I happened to glance over to the treadmill again. The owner of the gym, Chris, had stopped to talk to MacKenzie. He put his hand on her shoulder and leaned in. My stomach clenched again, and this time it had nothing to do with the earlier hit.

Cade took advantage of my newfound ADD and knocked me off my feet. Dragging in a deep gulp of air, I tried to fend off the sting of pain I knew was coming.

MacKenzie

"Shit," I shouted as I jumped off the treadmill and ran to grab my medic bag from the office.

Cade had hooked Ian in the jaw, sending him to the mat. I'd only been working at the gym for a month, but I'd never seen Ian fall before. I was so shocked, it took me a second to realize why I was rushing over to him. He was still on the mat when I got there, awake and wincing at the ceiling.

"Ian," I said, my voice unsteady. I put my hand on his chest, which rose and fell rapidly from his heavy breathing, then leaned over him. "Ian, are you okay?"

His eyes were open but he turned away, glaring at the wall as if he was pissed at something. When he finally turned up to look at me, his anger faded.

My breath caught. It was the first time I'd looked him in the eye since that night, and I couldn't believe how intense it was. He seemed so serious, and yet so in need of my touch, that before I could restrain myself I put my hand on his cheek, brushing his skin lightly with my thumb. His jaw was rough with stubble and sweaty from fighting. Heat zinged up my arm as memories flooded my brain.

"Are you hurt?" I asked, not sure why he hadn't yet responded. Maybe there was something wrong. "Ian?" My voice shook again as I moved to check the rest of his body, but he put up his gloved hand and turned my face back to his, making me lose myself in his eyes once more.

"I'm fine, Kenzie," he said in a low, raspy voice that made my insides melt. He took my hand in his and squeezed it gently. His fingerless gloves allowed the tips of his calloused fingers to scrape gently against the palm of my hand.

Then something changed in his eyes, and he pushed my hands away from him as he chuckled. "Don't worry, hon. I was just trying to give Cade a confidence boost."

He laughed, dropped my hand, and sat up. Ignoring me, he rubbed his hand over his short golden-brown hair as he looked at the floor, then turned his back to me and stood up.

What the...?

Then I remembered why I was mad at Ian, why I'd been burning him with icy glares ever since that night. The night that I didn't let myself think about.

"You really do think you're *all that*, don't you?" I said. "You don't need a nurse. Your injuries are all mental. I can't help you, you need a shrink." I got up and turned to walk away as I fought back tears.

Damn, I was such a baby. Why couldn't I just get over him? Why did I have to keep on getting pulled back in? Maybe I should have never taken this job. Of course, being near him was part of the draw, if I was being honest with myself.

The gym owner, Chris, came over and put an arm around me. "You okay, MacKenzie?"

I nodded and balled up my fists, digging my fingernails into my palms. It was a trick I'd learned to hold back the tears. I hated crying in front of people, showing them how weak I was. The pain of my nails biting into my skin pulled me out of the emotional drama and back to the real world.

"Sorry. I know I shouldn't bring my personal crap into work. It won't happen again." I moved to go, because I wanted to run to the bathroom and clean myself up, but Chris stopped me.

"Don't worry about it. You know you can talk to me right?" he asked.

I looked up at him. Chris had hired me last month, shortly after I was laid off from the hospital. Cade hooked me up with the interview, even though I was pretty sure it pissed Ian off that I was here. Chris interviewed me and after hiring me, had oriented me to the gym, but I still hadn't spent that much time with him.

Chris was in his late twenties. Before he was injured, he fought as a heavyweight, which meant he was the size of a frigging fridge. He needed a cane to walk now, but that didn't stop him from working out and keeping in shape. Whenever he had free time from his appointments, I'd find him working out. His shirt more than hinted at the firm muscles he maintained. His jawline was strong, and his head was shaved. I preferred my men with hair, but he wore it okay.

He gave me a smile. "Why don't we go out to lunch and you can tell me about it?"

IAN

Cade's punch had caught me by surprise, knocking me off-balance, and I couldn't recover my footing so I went down. But apart from a sore jaw and bruised ego, I would live. That didn't stop MacKenzie from rushing over to check on me.

She leaned over me, resting gentle fingers on my bare chest. Her long honey-colored hair brushed against my skin, and just like that, I was hers. Totally dumbstruck and hers. I couldn't even fucking talk.

But when my dick jumped up just as she turned to look at the rest of my body, I had to stop her. That was all I needed, for her to see me with a post-knockout boner. Here she was trying to make sure I wasn't hurt, and all I could do was get hard, as if she were some piece of meat. That made me just as bad as all the other turds at the gym. So I'd pulled her face back to look at me, only there was so much worry in her eyes, and all I wanted to do was take her in my arms and hold her and tell her I was okay.

God, I should have. I was an idiot. Why didn't I?

I knew she didn't want that, though. I traveled all the time for fights, and my career would always come first. Kenzie wanted more than I could offer, and she certainly deserved more. So I pushed her off. I turned and I sent her away, even though I knew she would be hurt. Somehow, I channeled the shit-bag in me and hurt her.

I was such a fucking dick.

And then Chris—I loved the guy, but he was a smooth bastard—was right there to pick up the pieces.

"Why don't we go out to lunch and you can tell me about it," Chris said. "Or we can talk about something else entirely, if you'd rather."

I held my breath, waiting for her answer. I wanted it to be no, but I knew it would be yes.

"Sure." She nodded.

"Great," Chris said. "We can—shoot. I have an important conference call this afternoon." He put his arm on her shoulder and said, "Let's make it dinner."

That made me want to hit something. Hard. I'd been hit so many times in my life, but nothing stung quite as much as hearing a friend ask out the girl you...

Okay, so I didn't know exactly what she was to me. And maybe that was for the best. It wasn't like Chris knew anything about me and her. Hell, it was probably a good thing that Chris asked her out; maybe now I could forget about Kenzie. Besides, I needed to focus on my upcoming fight. I didn't have time to worry about her. And Chris was a good guy. He would be good to her.

I could let her go. I should, even though it was the last thing I wanted to do.

Three

Would someone please tell me how the heck that happened?

One minute I was tending to Ian on the floor, and the next minute I was agreeing to go out with Chris, of all people. Sure, he was a nice guy, but I'd never thought of him that way. Not at all.

When he'd asked me to have lunch with him, of course I said yes. Because that was what you did when your boss asked you out for lunch. But then he switched it to dinner.

So here I was, walking by the river after dinner with my flipping boss. The night was cool and I had forgotten my sweater in his car, so I folded my arms in front of me to stay warm.

"Are you cold?" he asked.

I nodded. "A little."

He paused, took off his dinner jacket, and handed it to me. I shrugged it on. It was big and warm, and smelled strongly of Old Spice. A bit *too* strongly.

"Thanks." I started walking again, and Chris moved around me so that his cane was on the outside.

"Do you mind if I ask what happened?" I motioned toward his leg.

"No. Not at all. It was a fight." He paused, then chuckled. "Of course it was a fight."

"When did it happen?"

"Just over two years ago. I was on the fast track to becoming a pro fighter, and my manager lined me up with a guy—Billy Goat was his fighting name. He'd been fighting pro for a while, but because of the way he fought, my manager was sure I could take him. Heck, I was sure I could take him. Every defense weakness he had, I was strong at that offense. I should have won."

Chris stopped and leaned against the railing by the river. I wondered if his leg needed a break, or if he just wanted to stop and admire the view. So I stopped and leaned against the railing alongside him.

"What happened?"

"I was too cocky. I should have taken my time and waited for just the right moment to strike, but instead I went in fast and eager to get it done. I wore myself out in the first round, and by the second, I had become his punching bag."

I looked at Chris. He was a head taller than me, even in my six-inch heels. I couldn't imagine anyone turning him into a punching bag.

"He had me on the ground and was pummeling me. I should have tapped out of the fight and given it to him, but I wanted the win." He winced as if the memory of that moment pained him more than anything. "I managed to wrench my way out of his hold and get back up on my feet. I was so out of it at that point, I hardly remember a thing other than trying to remain standing. And then there was an insane pain as he came at my knee from the side, full force with his foot.

"His move was a foul, and lost him the fight. I won, but my knee refused to heal properly. I won the first and last fight of my pro career." He forced a chuckle, but it looked like he wasn't quite ready to laugh about the whole thing.

"Wow," I said. "You've tried physical therapy?"

"Too much scar tissue and not enough tendon left. It won't work right. I still do exercises with it, but it'll never be back to where it was."

He leaned forward and took my hand in his. For the first time that night, I didn't feel like I needed to pull away from him.

"It's all good, though. I found my calling. I opened up a gym, and it turns out I'm a much better trainer than I was a fighter."

Chris was a good trainer and well connected. I'd heard the guys at the gym talk about how his connections could help any good fighter work his way into the pro fighting circles.

I looked at him, inspecting his face. He had a mostly smooth complexion with a few freckles sprinkled across his slightly crooked nose. He couldn't be more than five years older than me, so he was maybe twenty-seven.

Could I like this guy? It had been a while since I'd dated anyone. I hadn't met anyone I really liked lately, but maybe I was just in a funk. Maybe I just needed to start dating again, and the liking, the wanting, would come. The way Chris looked at me told me he was more than game if I was.

"I just secured Ian his first pro fight," Chris said, his eyes lighting up with pride.

My heart filled with pride too. Pride for Ian, who'd been working so hard for this, and he would finally get his break. "That's great," I said.

"It's still two and a half months away, but we'll be heading to Vegas before you know it."

My mind flooded with thoughts of Ian. How would he feel when he heard the news? Most likely he'd play it off like it was no big deal. But he'd take this fight seriously and redouble his training so that when it came time for the fight, he'd be ready. I caught myself smiling at the thought.

Chris wove his fingers through mine and pulled me away from the wall. "Let's go grab a drink somewhere," he said smoothly, his eyes hooded.

A drink might loosen me up and help me stop my thoughts from constantly redirecting to Ian, but I was nervous that Chris would try to move too fast if we started drinking.

"I have to work in the morning," I said.

Chris chuckled. "I know your boss. Maybe I can talk to him and see if he'll let you come in late."

I stopped walking, making him stop too. "Chris…" I trailed off, not sure what I meant to say. "I don't want any special treatment." I let go of his hand. "I need this job, so I don't want this"—I pointed at each of us—"to get in the way of keeping my job. If you can do this, without being my boss, then I…"

God, what the hell was I trying to say?

He grabbed my hand again. "MacKenzie, don't worry about it. Don't even think about it. If it makes you feel better, when we're out, I'm not your boss. Anything that happens out here will not affect the way I treat you at the gym."

I nodded. It sounded like it could work. "Okay, sure," I said. "So, like, say I pushed you into the river right now, would I still have a job tomorrow?"

He chuckled at the ridiculousness of my being able to push him anywhere. "Of course. Your boss wouldn't hold that against you. And if you went out with me for a drink tonight, he would still expect you to show up tomorrow morning at nine a.m. sharp."

"Sorry, not tonight, but maybe another time?" I smiled.

"Another night, then."

We came back to his car and the alarm chirped. I wasn't the chivalry police, but I still couldn't help but notice that he was in the car before I had even opened the passenger door. I tried not to let it bug me.

As Chris drove, I pulled at the hem of my dress. The bucket seats of his Mustang kept tugging the skirt up, insistent on giving him a show. The A-line black dress that came down just past my knees was cute, but modest, or so I'd thought.

He had club music playing so loudly it shook the car, but turned it down when he pulled up in front of my building.

"So, MacKenzie, are you sure you don't want to get a drink?"

I didn't, but I had psyched myself up to let him kiss me good night, so he'd better hurry up and do it before I ran. "Sorry. Not tonight."

"All right," he said. "I had a great time."

"Me too. Thanks for dinner."

He leaned in close. I meant to let him kiss me, I really did, but I turned my face at the last second and he planted a wet, slow peck on my cheek.

Ugh. What am I, in sixth grade?

"Thanks." I ran from the car and let myself into the building without looking back.

Four

My apartment wasn't in the safest part of town, but I'd lived in worse when I was in foster care, so I didn't think about it too much. The paint-chipped stairwells with loose railings and creaky steps were in a secure building, which meant that I only had to deal with the few losers who lived inside the building itself—a small trade-off to be able to live in an apartment larger than a closet. After student loan payments, a closet was about all I'd be able to afford in a nicer part of town.

Still, I sometimes got creeped out at night when I walked through the dimly lit halls alone. Tonight was one of those times. I rushed up the stairs to my door and scrambled to get the key into the lock.

"Hey, MacKenzie."

I jumped but instantly recognized the raspy voice of Soni, the older lady who lived one door down.

"Hey, Soni," I said.

"Early night again?" she asked through the small crack in her door.

"Yeah," I said. "'Night."

Inside my apartment, I kicked off my heels and flopped down on the couch. Soni's words rang in my ears. *Early night again?*

What the hell did it say about me when an old woman thought I was having an early night? But she was right; I used to go out every night and stay out late. If it wasn't an all-nighter at the hospital, it was an all-nighter at the club. Lately I'd been feeling like I wanted more. As if maybe I could find someone more permanent in my life.

Could Chris be that person? Not if I didn't figure out how to pull it together.

And I really needed to pull it together.

Except that I couldn't. I'd always been a bit of a wild girl, never been able to grasp the whole get-married-and-have-a-baby thing.

I blamed it on my upbringing. I'd lived in no fewer than twenty different foster homes as a kid. None of them were as crazy as the ones you read about in books. I knew I was lucky; I'd never been sexually abused, and was only hit once by a foster dad, from whose care I was promptly removed. But none of the families I stayed with ever connected with me emotionally or had time for me, so I got used to being alone.

When I started dating, I never figured out how to stay with one guy for long. A quick night or two of fun, then run before they had a chance to hurt me. That was my MO. But something about that night with Ian—I wasn't sure exactly what, but something changed.

The night was supposed to be about Alexa and Cade. Alexa had dubbed it their coming-out party. I'd known they were going to end up together from the start. Or I was pretty sure anyway.

For me, the night was less about them and more about Cade's hot cage-fighter friend, Ian. Alexa was sure I'd seen him before, but I knew I'd remember meeting someone that delish. By the way I caught him looking at me, I'd known the night had the potential to be one neither of us would forget.

And it was. I still remembered it like it was yesterday, though the memory was tinged with a mixture of sadness and longing.

I fell asleep thinking about it…

****

Ian had crowded in next to me in the booth. The club had been loud, so we'd sat close in order to hear each other over the music.

"So, are you a porn star too?" I had asked. Cade had only ever done two movies, but I couldn't resist the temptation.

Ian choked on his drink, roughly swallowing the gulp. "Um, no."

"Don't have the balls for it, huh?" I teased, fighting off a smile.

His eyes narrowed on mine, and his mouth lifted in a playful smirk. "My package is more than adequate, if that's what you're asking."

I licked my lips and leaned closer. "Then what are you afraid of? I heard the money's great." Something in me liked teasing him; he seemed too in control, too domineering, and I wanted to ruffle his feathers.

"I guarantee I'd outlast and out measure every man on that porn set. I don't because I choose not to."

I dropped my head back, laughing. "Sure, sure."

Ian pressed closer, aligning his face with mine so he could peer straight into my eyes as he spoke. "Some things are private. And my cock is reserved for my wife."

"You're married?" My gaze dropped to recheck his left hand, which I already knew was ringless.

"My future wife," he clarified.

How noble of him. "Wait. Do you mean you're saving yourself for marriage?"

He shook his head. "I'm no virgin, but I'm sure my future bride wouldn't like knowing I'd fucked everything from here to New York, and filmed it. You know?"

I nodded, suddenly losing my playful edge. He was right. And he was sweet. I wasn't expecting that.

We spent the next two hours talking and laughing, the topics ranging from innocuous things like our favorite pizza toppings, to more serious subjects like how many children we wanted to have. He wanted two; I was undecided.

His eyes flashed his confusion, but before I had time to explain about my foster-care upbringing and my reluctance to bring kids into a less-than-perfect situation, Alexa leaned over from across the table. "Dance with me, Kenzie."

"Sure," I said and turned to Ian. "Join us?"

He looked over to Cade, who was comfortable where he was in the booth. Ian and I might have just met, but we both knew Cade didn't like to dance.

"I'll sit this one out." Ian's eyes were on mine, and I got the impression he was fighting an urge to come dance with me.

I hated to leave him there. Our connection, even though it was only hours old, had been so much deeper than I had ever felt before. But Lexa was dying to dance, so I got up.

Ian moved back and I slipped out past him. For a moment, my breasts were almost in his face, and yet he didn't break eye contact with me. A warm ripple of pleasure shot through me.

The music was so loud, my entire body buzzed with every thump of the bass. Out on the dance floor with Alexa, I swayed my hips, letting the music guide me. God, I loved to dance. I lost myself completely in the music until I wasn't moving to the song anymore, the song was moving me.

I was so lost in it that I hardly noticed when someone came up behind me and started grinding with me. I turned to see who it was, expecting it to be Alexa, but it was some drunk kid just messing around. I laughed and shrugged, dancing with him. The kid was all wiry and bony, definitely not my type. But I was all about having a good time, and just because I danced with him didn't mean I had to go home with him.

But then he grabbed my ass, and before I had the chance to tell him to stop, Ian materialized and pulled him away. They faced off in front of me, barely a foot apart. Ian was taller than my dance partner, with five times the muscle, but he was also the cooler of the two. His body was tense, but his eyes maintained their usual calm and cool control.

The drunk guy lunged at Ian, which made me chuckle until I realized that Ian could probably kill him without breaking a sweat.

Ian grabbed the guy's hand in one of his own, twisting it so the guy was forced to bend over or break his wrist. Meanwhile, Ian had hardly moved, his face still calm and collected. Then Ian bent down to the guy's ear and said a few things I couldn't hear. The man nodded, Ian released him, and he staggered away, hugging his wrist to his body.

When Ian turned back to me, his jaw was tense and his nostrils flared. His gaze penetrated me in ways that made my body burn. Knowing he'd just stood up for me lit some fire inside me. As far as I was concerned, that was the hottest thing a man could do, mental foreplay in my book.

I moved toward him, needing to be closer. Ian didn't break eye contact as he pulled me into his arms and pressed our bodies together, making my pulse spike. His body was so amazingly rock hard, and yet perfectly shaped for me to fit against him.

The next song was slower, and we adjusted our hips and moved to the music. I brought my arms up around his neck, and he lifted me up so that our faces were inches apart. I wrapped my legs around his waist. Ian held me to him, looking into my eyes for a long moment.

When he leaned in and brushed his lips against mine, I was so glad he was already holding me up, because my body went completely limp. His lips were tender even as he took control of the kiss, first nipping playfully at my lips, but then opening my mouth with his and moving his tongue against mine.

His arms moved from my waist down to my hips, and then his hands cupped my ass as he pressed me to him. I gasped. His rock-hard cock pressed against my center. The only barriers between us were his jeans and my wet panties. I squeezed my legs around him and pressed against him harder, wondering if it was possible to break him in half with my legs. As an extreme fighter, I was pretty sure he'd survive, although if I didn't have him soon, I thought I might die.

Ian's eyes met mine as the club around us faded into the background. Nothing else existed but the raw need inside me. With his gaze firmly locked onto mine, he read every thought buzzing through my brain, and the dark, hungry look in his eyes told me we were on the same page. He'd been so easy to talk to, so open, and made me feel at ease. And now he was pressing close to me, letting me feel every hard inch of him. I wanted more.

I didn't know how we got to his car, but damn, I had been so happy when I saw it that I'd flipping squealed. He had dug his keys out of his pocket and opened the back door, guiding me into the backseat...

******

I woke up with a gasp, my breath coming in pants. I dreamed about that night often, and the throbbing ache between my legs needed to be taken care of.

Now.

I had a vibrator, but knew from experience that after waking up from one of these dreams, I hardly had to touch myself, I was already so close to the edge. Taking a deep breath, I closed my eyes again and imagined what it would have been like if Ian had followed me into the backseat of his car and closed the door, if he had pulled me forward and spread my legs.

My finger circled between my thighs, and I imagined Ian's smoldering eyes locked on mine as he ripped off my wet panties. Frantic, I'd hurry to open the front of his jeans. He'd pull his pants down just enough to free his cock, which I knew would be huge and hard. He'd slide a finger inside me, and when he felt how hot and ready I was, he'd climb over me and thrust into me so hard I'd cry out and come apart instantly.

He'd hold himself still as the wave of spasms rocked through my body and then slowed. Then he'd slowly pull out and push inside me again, and as he increased his pace, he'd wrap his arms around me, pulling me close and holding me tight.

I'd shiver from the sheer pleasure of it, and run my hands over his rock-hard back muscles up to his shoulders as he moved faster, pushing harder and harder. Then he'd slip his hand down and lightly press a thumb on my throbbing clit. My nails would dig into his back as I came apart again, crying his name.

A real orgasm tore through me at that point, just like it always did. As I came down from my self-induced, Ian-inspired release, I was again reminded of how that night had actually ended...

****

That night we'd kissed frantically on the dance floor, and he'd carried me out to his car as we pressed together in heated passion.

But when he guided me into the backseat, he didn't follow me as he should have. Instead, he promptly backed away from the car with a tight look on his face that I couldn't quite read. Then he closed the door, leaving me more alone than I had felt in a long time.

I was hurt at first, but then I got angry, like terror-alert-level-orange angry. Was I not good enough for him? I fumbled with the door handle until I opened it and got out.

"What the hell?" I snapped.

"I'm sorry," he said as he shook his head and ran a hand over his hair. "I just can't do this."

"Why not? There aren't any cameras here. This isn't an adult movie shoot that your 'future wife' might see, so what's the problem?"

"Get in the car. I'll take you home." His expression shuttered and I could no longer read his face, as if he'd cut me off not just physically, but emotionally.

"What the hell was that?" I said. "I thought we were going to have some fun. What happened?"

He shook his head and looked away. "Nothing, I just shouldn't have started this in the first place. I don't have time for this right now, I have a fight in two days. I need to stay focused." He wouldn't look me in the eyes anymore.

Did he just say he didn't have time for this? For me? Familiar negative emotions came roaring back before I could stop them. I felt like I'd been punched.

I was used to this by now, to people not having time for me. I'd been dealing with this all my life. But for some reason, hearing it from Ian hurt more than it had in a long time. I thought we'd made a real connection. He'd come to my rescue on the dance floor and had been sweet and easy to talk to.

Stunned, I'd realized that despite my checkered past, I'd never felt quite so rejected before. So I'd dug my fingernails into the palms of my hands, but the pain couldn't stop the stupid tears.

Without another word, I had rushed to a nearby taxi stand, got in the back of the first one, and slammed the door.

Five

The office at the gym was smaller than my own at home, but Chris had managed to squeeze in a dingy cracked-leather sofa, along with an old desk and bulky chair. I tossed my bag in the corner and shoved a pile of towels off the couch to make room.

Chris reached behind his desk and pulled a protein shake out of his mini fridge, then tossed it to me. "Heads up, bro."

I caught it and shook it before unscrewing the cap. The shit was green and thick, which no drink should *ever* be. It tasted like blended dirt and leaves. I took a deep breath and chugged it down in as few gulps as I could manage.

I shuddered. Even though I drank the same nasty breakfast every morning, I never got used to it. It was just one of the many brutal things I willingly put myself through, because it took sacrifice to become a pro MMA fighter. And knowing I was close to achieving my dream fueled me to keep pushing.

"I had a call yesterday with Shannon," Chris said, and I perked up. Steve Shannon was the manager of several pro fighters. If I could get a match, even with one of his newer fighters, I would be almost there. "He wants you to fight Gator. He's set it up already for two months from now."

"Gator," I repeated. There were several pro fighters in my weight class I thought I could beat, and he was one of them.

Game on.

"He's a wrestler, so we'll need to work on your ground technique. I've got a guy coming into town next week to train with you."

Without Chris, I wouldn't be where I was now. I was a good fighter, but it wasn't just about fighting, it was about who you trained with and who you knew. Chris knew everyone, all the managers and all the coaches. He also knew enough fighters that I often ended up training with pros. It sounded like he had another one lined up. *Good.* I needed someone to challenge me.

Through the one-way glass, I could see MacKenzie as she jumped on the treadmill for her morning run.

"Where'd you take her?" I asked. I hadn't meant to ask Chris about his night with Kenzie, but I couldn't stand not knowing. What was it about her that made me lose control?

"Zito's," was his one-word answer.

Shit. I gave him the perfect opportunity to spill the details, and he didn't take it. I'd spent all last night beating myself up about the two of them out together. Alone. I wanted them to go and have a good time. I wanted Kenzie to have fun. I kept on telling myself that.

But I knew Chris. I knew he liked to bag them as soon as he possibly could. And the thought of him touching her made me really glad I wasn't juicing, because I already wanted to pound him just for the image that put in my mind. So I'd promised myself I wouldn't ask, and hopefully he wouldn't tell me.

Only he always told, so why wasn't he talking now? Could it be that nothing actually happened?

I looked out at her on the treadmill. God, I wanted to know so bad I almost flat-out asked him if he fucked her. *Get a grip, Ian.*

"That's a pretty high-end restaurant," I said instead. Because it was, for him. Normally a girl was lucky if he took her to an all-you-can-eat buffet.

"I was in the mood for something different." Chris shrugged. "Besides, MacKenzie is different."

Damn right, she was. I took a deep breath. Something about the way he said that, though, got under my skin. There was only one thing worse than them having sex, or maybe just as bad—

He could be falling for her.

"You're cool with me dating her, right?" he asked. "You don't have anything going with her, do you?"

"No." The word felt like sawdust in my mouth. "It's fine. Just be careful, she's Cade's girl's best friend. They're like family. So don't fuck with her."

The last part might have come out a bit more venomous than I'd intended. Too fucking bad. When it came to MacKenzie, something inside me needed to make sure she'd be treated right.

Chris lifted his chin in acknowledgment. "Like I said, she's different. I think I could actually like her. Hey, speaking of women, when's the last time you saw some action?" He broke out into a big smile, and I wanted to pound him. Again.

"Dick," I said.

He was fucking with me, but it was no joke, I needed a good ground-and-pound with a coed. Maybe that would get my mind off MacKenzie. Besides, I was getting serious blue balls from all the sex I was *not* having. Another sacrifice I made while in training mode.

Sex was a distraction. One that I desperately wanted, but couldn't afford. There was an important fight in just under a week. I was the sure bet, but my opponent actually had a chance. And that meant I had to be on top of it. I had to win. My dick would have to wait his turn.

"I'm gonna go suit up," Chris said, then got up to leave. "See you out there."

On his way out, he stopped briefly to talk to MacKenzie. She smiled at him, then laughed at something he said. I couldn't help but notice the smile didn't reach her eyes.

He headed to the locker room, leaving MacKenzie on the treadmill. It wouldn't hurt to sit and take in the view. Besides, I had a few minutes.

Give up the chance to watch her run? I might be in training mode, but I was still a man.

Six

I knew this double-date thing was a bad idea, but I couldn't explain why. Chris had a way of talking me into things without me even realizing it, so here I was, getting ready for yet another date with him. A double date with Ian, no less.

I downed a glass of chardonnay—my get-ready-to-go-out drink of choice—as I stood over my bed, trying to figure out which dress to wear. It was down to the navy blue dress with a flowing skirt and a modest scoop-neck top, or the skintight wine-colored spaghetti-strap number.

Glancing at the clock, I sighed. Chris was due to pick me up any second now. I needed to make a decision.

Screw it. If Ian was coming with a date, it didn't matter anymore. I was going to wear the sexiest thing I had, and he could just see what he was missing.

Stepping into the skintight dress, I pulled it up. The buzzer rang as I slid into my shoes. I took one last swig of wine and hopped out the door, pulling my second shoe on as I struggled to maintain the hold on my clutch. I skipped down the stairs and out the door, slamming right into Chris.

"Well, hello," he said as he stumbled back, catching us both. "You in a hurry, sweetie?"

He smiled and looked down at my face, then he looked down farther. My cleavage appeared to have gained his attention.

Fine. Let him look. I tried to convince myself that I wanted to date Chris; maybe it was time for me to shit or get off the pot, or whatever. I stumbled a little and hiccupped.

"Oops. Hi, Chris," I said, my voice coming out higher than normal.

He took my arm, steadying me. "You're starting a little early tonight, don't you think?"

"I may have had a little too much getting-ready wine," I explained, my face hot. Yep, definitely too much. "Sorry."

"It's okay, sweetie." Chris kissed me on the lips. This was our third date, but only our first lip-on-lip kiss. It was close-mouthed and he came in a little too hard, as if he was worried I would back away before he could follow through. "Let's get going," he said, then led me to the car.

The restaurant wasn't that far, but the buzz I had from the wine was wearing off by the time we got there.

Ian and his date were already seated when we arrived. The table was quiet as we approached, and they looked as if they hadn't been talking much. Ian was a little stiff, but put on a smile when he saw us. His date was drop-dead flipping gorgeous. Of course she was; she was with Ian, for goodness' sake.

I was seated across from her. God, why? She had long legs and looked like a swimsuit model.

She smiled. "Hi, I'm Sara." It was a genuine smile. Which made me hate her, of course. Her hair was beautiful, long and flowing red locks. She looked familiar, though.

It hit me so suddenly that I barely managed to stifle a small, "Oh shit," as I covered my mouth.

It was *her*. Cade's first adult movie co-star. Desiree was her stage name, but we called her "the screamer" because she'd howled like a banshee through the whole thing. It sounded so fake, it was painful.

The night we'd gathered around Alexa's laptop and watched Cade's video came flooding back. I struggled to keep a straight face, but could hardly look "Sara" in the eyes, even as I couldn't stop staring at her.

"Nice to meet you, *Sara*," I said. I hadn't meant to emphasize her name, but it came out that way. I gave her as friendly a smile as I could manage before turning to Ian and Chris. "Should we get a bottle of wine?"

"Yes," Sara and Ian both answered at the same time.

Chris looked at Ian, shocked.

Ian smiled. "I mean for you guys, yeah. I'm in training mode. I have my water." He pointed at his glass on the table.

When the waiter arrived with a bottle of white, we filled our glasses. The conversation turned to Ian's next fight in just two days with a semi-pro fighter named Steel.

"Remember, he's a ground fighter," Chris said. "Keep him on his feet, and he's your bitch."

Ian leaned in and the two of them began strategizing, leaving Sara and me to listen.

Curious, I watched how Ian was with Sara. They had almost a foot of space between them. I looked over to see how far Chris was from me; it was about the same. Not that I was keeping score or anything.

Chris glanced at me and leaned closer, taking my hand. "So, Sara," he said. "What is it that you do?"

"She's a graphic designer," Ian said quickly. She looked at him and nodded.

Why was Ian lying about what she did for a living?

"Really?" I asked after taking another sip of wine. "Where do you work?"

"She does freelance," Ian answered for her again.

I blotted my lips with my napkin and placed it on my plate. "I have to go to the ladies' room." Then I grabbed my clutch and pulled my phone out, dialing Alexa as I walked.

"Did you know Ian was dating the screamer?" I didn't even give Alexa time to answer before I started. My phone pressed to my ear, I made it to the back hallway near the restrooms, but didn't go in, choosing to loiter outside instead.

There was a pause. "I'm not sure they're actually dating," Alexa answered when she figured out what I was ranting about. "Cade warned me that she would be going out with Ian. He wanted to know if I would be okay with it. He posed it as a favor to Ian, like he was setting them up for some reason."

"Why on earth would Ian need to be set up on a blind date? He's amazing." It slipped out, and I couldn't put it back in. *Damn wine.*

"Yeah," she said, then paused. "But there's something else weird about the whole thing. Cade asked me—no, *begged* me not to tell you that she was a porn star." She giggled through the phone. "I didn't have the heart to remind him that you'd seen the movie too."

"Oh my God, Lexa!"

I couldn't believe what she was saying. Did Ian really not want me to know he was dating a porn star? Why?

"Why does he care what I think of his sexploits? He can fuck any porn star he damn well pleases."

The second I said the words "porn star," I noted two things. First, I was definitely talking too loudly, and second, "Sara" had rounded the corner and was within earshot.

So I did what any stupid idiot who'd just stuck their foot in their mouth would do—I pretended it didn't happen. I ducked my head and walked past Sara without looking her in the eye, the phone still pressed to my ear as I headed back to the table.

"It seemed important to Cade, so I hope you won't tell," Alexa said.

"Who is there left to tell? Chris?"

Maybe that was it. Ian didn't want Chris to know because Chris would tease him about it later. I didn't know why, but the thought of telling Chris wasn't appealing to me.

"Their secret is safe with me," I whispered. "Look, sweetie, I gotta go."

Then I sat back down at the table.

Seven

I'd never hired a prostitute, and had never paid for sex. Hell, I never had to. So when I asked Cade if he knew anyone I could bring out on a double date with Chris and MacKenzie, I wasn't expecting him to suggest paying someone. Still, once I'd heard him out, his idea didn't seem totally whack. In fact, it made sense.

Normally I would have brought one of the gym bunnies to the dinner, because all I needed was a pretty girl on my arm, but the big fight was only two days away and I didn't trust myself. I'd become one serious horndog, and it seemed to get exponentially worse whenever MacKenzie was around.

So I needed a sure thing. Someone I could trust to *not* throw herself at me.

Cade's friend Sara was on her own and trying to take care of a newborn. My trust fund was pretty well padded, so we settled on the terms: a few hundred dollars and a free meal in exchange for her company for the evening.

"Thanks for coming out tonight," I said as I drove Sara home.

"Sorry I was so quiet," she said. "I guess I'm not good at this escort business."

"It was fine. You were great," I lied.

She'd looked on edge for most of the night, but Chris didn't seem to notice and MacKenzie was sauced, so I didn't know how she would have known. All that mattered was that the night was finally fucking over. I could pay Sara and never think of her again.

"I feel like I could have been better if I was alone with you," she said.

"What the—"

My tires squealed and I nearly ran off the road when she grabbed my dick. What the fucking fuck was I paying her for? I had made it very clear when I picked her up that I was *not* paying for sex. *No extras.*

"No," I said as I lifted her hand out of my lap and put it back in her own where it belonged. "I told you, I just needed a date for the dinner. I don't need any of that."

"You're telling me a guy like you doesn't need this?"

She picked up my hand and stuck my middle finger in her mouth, all the way in, sucking it hard and licking at it with her tongue. I couldn't help imagining her hot, wet mouth on my cock, and I almost pulled the fuck over right there. This girl definitely knew what she was doing. *Goddamn.*

But training mode was training mode.

"I can't. I told you we wouldn't. I'm sorry if you misunderstood the deal. I'm training." I pulled my finger out of her mouth and wiped her saliva on my pants. *Yuck.* And my dick went soft.

Sara pulled her mouth into a little pout. "Sorry, I know you said no sex, but I wasn't going to charge you or anything. I just…" She shook her head and looked out the window. "Never mind. Sorry."

The rest of the ride back to her apartment was damn awkward. I was tempted to peel off as soon as she was out of my car, but I had to go inside and pick up my little sister, Sophia, who'd been babysitting Sara's baby so that she could go out.

Sara fumbled with the lock, pushing and pulling at the door before it finally burst open, and I could see inside the tiny front room of her apartment. Sophia was there on the sofa just as I'd figured she would be, but the person next to her, Cade's former adult film producer, I never thought I'd see again. And I sure as fuck didn't ever want to see him in the same room with my little sister. Every single muscle in my body tensed instantly.

Fighting outside the ring was a bad idea for any serious fighter. It could lead to serious injury—of the other party, of course—and then there were all the rules intended to keep everyone safe in the ring. But they didn't apply out here.

Sophia sprang up the second she saw me come in. Her eyes widened and she scurried back toward the kitchen. "We were just talking," she said, as if I would be okay with my little sister talking to a pornography producer. I didn't care if it was the softer stuff; stay the fuck away from Sophia.

I clenched my jaw and breathed deeply, trying to stay calm enough to not murder this little shit.

He stood up with a friendly-ass grin on his face, seemingly oblivious to the fact that I was a hair away from redecorating Sara's apartment with his internal organs, and took a step toward me.

"Hey, Ian, remember me? I'm Rick. I was just stopping in to check on Sara."

He was most likely there to try to talk Sara into coming back to work for him, but Cade told me she'd been out of the business for a while and was planning on staying that way. The bit about her being a designer wasn't a total lie; she was going to school to be one, she just hadn't finished yet.

It didn't matter what reason Rick had for being here, though. He was not welcome. As soon as I got my rage partially under control, I stepped toward him. "I think you'd better leave."

"I was just checking in on—"

"Rick, go." Sophia interrupted him, her voice urgent. She knew me, and knew I wasn't dicking around.

"Don't you worry, sweet little Sophia. I'm just—" Rick started, but I didn't let him finish.

I swept his feet out from under him, then grabbed his hand and twisted it, pulling him backward toward the door so that he had to scurry crablike after me in order to not break his wrist.

"You didn't know Sophia was my little sister, which is the only reason I'm not killing you right now. Get the fuck out, and never come back." I pulled him out the door and left him in the hallway. "If you ever approach Sophia again…" I didn't finish because, hell, who knew what I'd do if I ever saw him with Sophia again.

Rick looked seriously pissed off as I slammed the door on him. *Tough shit.*

"Sophia, what the hell were you doing talking to that shit-bag?"

My sister folded her arms over her chest and glared up at me. "Ian, you can't tell me who to talk to. You don't get to do that to everyone."

"The hell I don't. If I ever catch him near you again, it's his fucking funeral. Now, grab your stuff and let's go." I pulled out a wad of cash and thrust it into Sara's hand on my way to the door.

"Damn it, Ian," Sophia said as she grabbed her purse, but she followed me out.

I never should have had her watch Sara's kid. I knew Sara was a former "actress." It was my own fault Sophia was here.

"You know what he does, right?" I asked Sophia as I drove her home.

"Yeah." She looked at me like I was a total shit. She knew she was the only person who could look at me that way and get away with it. "He's Cade's adult film director."

Sophia wiped her hand across her nose and turned to look out the window, her knee bouncing rapidly up and down. She did that when she was pissed off.

I left her alone and drove her back to her apartment in silence.

Eight

I knew that, as a nurse, I shouldn't enjoy watching two guys beat on each other so much, but it was cage fighting. All that raw testosterone being thrown around was a total turn-on. And let's not forget that these guys were naked from the waist up, and totally built.

Um, and maybe I pretended they were fighting over me.

My eyes were fixed on the guy in blue shorts. Sweat dripped from his face onto his firm bronzed pecs. His body was already glistening. It was the final round, and he was still throwing punches and kicks. He'd lost some of the bounce in his step, but his opponent sagged on his feet, his eyes half closed. He was in a perpetual block stance with his hands in front of his face, probably just hoping he could stay standing until the final horn.

It looked like Sweaty Pecs was going to win this one. To be honest, it wasn't the most exciting fight I'd seen.

I stifled a yawn and nudged Ty. "Watch, you pussy." He was curled up on his folding chair, peeking through the cracks between his fingers.

"Kenzie, I can't believe you can watch this. You are one sick chick."

"Why did you come if you didn't want to see them fight?" I asked. I knew why, but I still liked to tease him. Ty was so newly out of the closet that he had a hard time saying it aloud sometimes.

"I like watching them when they're sparring. I thought this would be like that," he said, his voice high and whiny.

"You just wanted to get your fill of shirtless men. Admit it. But why can't you get into it? Pretend one of them is fighting for your honor." I batted my eyelashes at him.

He bit his lower lip, and his gaze wandered as he considered the implications.

I laughed. The guys at the gym were gay friendly, but they were also mostly very straight. The idea of being in a relationship with a guy would probably make them get huffy pretty damn quick.

Ian entered the room and took a seat off to the side of the ring. His fight was up next, the main event. He sat up straight, his muscles relaxed even as he watched the fight closely, as if it was an important lesson. His eyes followed every move of each fighter. You could almost see him mentally taking notes of what the fighter was doing well, and more importantly, where his vulnerabilities were.

He was so intently watching the fight that I could safely look at him without him noticing. A hint of his eight-pack rippled under his T-shirt. His arms were tanned, but not yet sweaty. His skin looked soft, and I knew his muscles were rock hard.

The final buzzer sounded, pulling my attention away from Ian and back to the cage. Sweaty Pecs won by judges' decision.

"Woo-hoo!" I shouted, nudging Ty, who'd managed to at least put his feet down on the floor.

"MacKenzie." Chris smiled as he beckoned me up to the cage.

"That's me," I said and grabbed my medic bag, heading to the front.

Voices buzzed excitedly as everyone milled around, getting ready for the main event, and I moved to the side to do my post-fight check. First with the loser; sadly, he was one of ours. He was exhausted, dehydrated, and would be bruised as shit tomorrow, but he'd survive.

Next, I looked over the winner. "What's your name?" I asked as I shined a light in his eyes to check for reaction.

"I'm Adam," he said.

"Nice fight tonight, Adam," I said as I took his pulse. This was all routine. As the gym medic, I checked all the fighters after amateur bouts like this one.

As I tracked the second hand on my watch, another fighter stepped up behind my patient. *Nice abs.* I licked my lips and looked up to see who it was, and tried not to show how annoyed I was as I inwardly rolled my eyes. It was Ian. Mr. Porn-star-dater himself.

"Hi, MacKenzie," he said stiffly.

He sounded all formal. *So irritating.* If he didn't want to be with me, that was fine, but I didn't need this stupid professional crap between us.

I didn't respond, instead turning back to my patient. "Do you feel like you sustained any injuries?" I knew from watching the fight that he would be sore tomorrow, but there was nothing serious.

"I think I may have pulled my groin muscle," he said as he smiled and winked at me. "Could you take a look?"

Ian remained rooted to the spot behind Adam, his head cocked as he waited to see how I would respond.

What I did next was totally insane. "Sure," I said as I smiled at him sweetly and slid my hand up his thigh.

What the crap am I doing? His thigh was rock hard but he wasn't that hot, and we were in the middle of the gym. Chris's gym. Chris, who I was dating.

I caught the rage in Ian's posture, though, and that egged me on. I gave Adam my best doe-eyed smile and grabbed his groin protector. His cock hardened quickly, and he moved to adjust his jewels.

"Does that hurt?" I asked innocently.

When Ian let out a huge breath and stormed off, I stifled a laugh and stood up. *Serves you right, you big jerk. Hurts, doesn't it?*

"Hey," Adam said. "You aren't done examining my injuries."

"You'll be fine," I said and turned to go back to my seat, but Adam grabbed my arm.

"Hey, slut, you started something."

I barely had time to react before Chris was in front of Adam, all puffed up and ready to go. He might not fight anymore, but he could still whip any guy at the gym, even with his bum knee. Most guys knew this, and even if Adam didn't, he should be able to see that Chris had about a hundred more pounds of muscle on him than Adam's slight featherweight build.

The gym owner didn't say a word. He just stared at Adam until he backed down, grabbing his gear bag and heading to the exit.

Chris then turned to me with a disgusted sneer. "Does he think just because he wins a fight he can grab any reward he wants?"

"Yeah," I said and ran my hand through my hair. I shouldn't have grabbed Adam that way, but in that moment, I wanted to get at Ian riled up so bad, I went for it. There was no way in hell I would admit any of this to Chris, though, so I just agreed.

"I've got your back, sweetie," he said, then leaned down and kissed me on the nose.

"Thanks, boss."

I kept my voice even but gave him a pointed look, reminding him of the deal we'd made. I was just a medic when we were at work. The dating thing only went on outside the gym. Then I headed back to my folding chair in the first row.

Ty seemed to have forgotten he was scared of fighting and was finally getting into the half-naked-man show going on, which was exactly why I'd brought him. He was like a girlfriend without the competition…so flipping awesome!

Ian's opponent stepped into the ring and immediately started dancing around with his fists in the air. To my surprise, a good portion of the audience cheered for him. I looked around; maybe this guy had a few friends in the audience.

One of the refs checked over Ian, then let him into the ring as well.

"Ladies and gentlemen," the announcer began. "This is the main event, three five-minute rounds, middleweight MMA fight. Weighing in at one hundred ninety pounds, twenty-four-year-old Ian Leclaire, representing the home gym. His opponent, twenty-seven-year-old Michael Steel, weighing in at two hundred pounds, hailing from Las Vegas."

From the few fights I'd seen, Ian had been fighting below his potential for a while. It seemed like every fight he had, he ended up knocking the guy out in the first round. I'd heard he once knocked someone out with the first punch.

The fight tonight was supposed to be different, though. This guy Steel had fought pro before, if only somewhat briefly. But if Ian could win this fight, it would open all kinds of doors for him. I was already on the edge of my seat.

Inside the ring, the ref talked to the fighters briefly before he had them touch gloves and the first round started. Ian was a bouncer; he jumped around on his feet. Steel shook his head as if trying to shake a voice from his mind, then he stepped in to swing at Ian.

Ian was ready for him and sidestepped as he jabbed the guy squarely in the jaw. Steel jerked back. I thought I was about to watch Ian's second ever one-hit knockout, but Steel found his footing and only wavered slightly before he came back at Ian. Hard.

"Damn, girl," Ty said.

"What?" I turned to him.

"You just totally flinched."

"I did not. You're crazy."

"*Tsk*. Whateves."

Nine

IAN

Adrenaline rushed through my veins, and I couldn't have that. Too much adrenaline too soon, and you tired yourself out.

It was stupid of me to try to engage with Kenzie before a fight. Now I just wanted to hit something, hard. But this guy was a pro, and it would take more than just brute force to win this. I needed skill and a level head.

We touched gloves, and I went right for the obvious jaw jab without even thinking. *Damn.* I wasn't supposed to do that. The guy's skull was so thick, he'd never been knocked out. I knew this, but I couldn't focus.

Must focus.

I bounced on my toes to bleed the energy out and to try to keep him guessing, but then I lost it and came at him. One punch, then another, then a kick. He blocked both punches, then he blocked my kick. I went at him again, punching at him over and over like a fucking idiot, but I couldn't stop, haunted by the scared look on Kenzie's face when Chris was holding that fighter back. What had he done to her?

Frustrated, I whaled on Steel some more, but he calmly blocked every blow. At the rate I was burning calories, I'd exhaust myself by the end of the first round. Yet I couldn't stop hitting him and kept at it until he finally threw a punch.

I jumped the wrong way, putting myself right in the line of fire. *Fuck.* Right on the nose. That was going to leave a mark.

"Get your ass in gear and move!" Chris called out from the sidelines. He knew I was distracted; he just didn't know it was because the idea of anyone messing with MacKenzie turned me into a homicidal maniac.

I bounced back and shook it off. The metallic taste in the back of my mouth told me I was bleeding, but I ignored it.

Steel bobbed in front of me, throwing punches I knew were fake because I was familiar with his fight style, I'd watched it so many times. I easily avoided his swings, remembering that he would soon try to grab me and bring me to the ground. I whirled before he got the chance and gave him a strong kick to the side of his head.

Contact.

His whole body floated sideways from my kick and fell into the cage wall.

Steel pushed himself back on his feet, and I went at him again. He really had lost some of his fight, almost falling as he came at me.

He raised his fists again, and I thought he was about to go for my kidney so I moved to block, but instead he punched me right in the fucking throat.

I spun back, grabbing at my throat as if that would get me the air that I needed. *Son of a bitch, that hurt.* I clutched the side of the cage and gasped for breath. A pinch of air, then another. I was breathing, sort of. The ref came over and put a hand on my shoulder, and I waved him off. I just needed some room so that I could breathe. *Please.*

Kenzie was suddenly right in front of me, grabbing the links of the cage as she stared at me, wide-eyed. I didn't want her getting close to Steel. I didn't want her anywhere near this shitball. I waved her off, or tried to. Stubbornly she held on, and Chris had to step in and pull her away.

"Are you okay?" the ref asked.

I nodded, but put my hand up between us to let him know I needed a second. It must have taken me too long, because he held up his hand as if he was about to announce the winner.

Fuck. I didn't want this. Steel's fist to the throat was a foul. And if I could no longer fight because of his move, I won.

He was about to announce my win, but I didn't want to win this way. It was like winning a pool game because the other guy scratched on the eight ball. It would say nothing about my skill level, only that Steel was a dirty fighter. I wouldn't get the recognition I needed, and I wouldn't get the new fights I wanted.

"Wait," I said, the word coming out scratchy because my voice didn't want to work. "I'm good," I whispered.

Damn, I sounded like shit, but as I spoke, my breath started to come more easily. The ref relented, and the fight was back on. My neck hurt like a bitch, but there was only fifty seconds left in this round. If I could just hang on until then, I might be able to win this. I hoped. *Fuck.*

I led with a kick and managed to corner him against the fence, pounding his face several times in rapid succession. He curled up to hide his face, and I punched him in the side. He sank to the floor, and I rolled him over and put a hold on him.

With a surprising burst of energy, Steel pushed back and rolled us over, landing all his weight on my shoulder. I heard the crunch. It hurt so bad, I fucking yelled. But I managed to pull him off with my other arm, wrap my legs around him, and secure the hold around his neck. He waited a beat before he tapped out.

Yeah, bitches!

The bell rang, and I let Steel up.

The crowd roared to its feet, but as I stood up, my shoulder screamed in pain. It hurt so badly, I pounded my fist into the cage, as if that would make the pain stop.

Kenzie was in the ring as soon as the fight was called. She stopped in front of me, her eyes all red and wet.

What? What happened? What made her cry? I didn't understand.

Ten

"Ty, you're not on a Sunday drive. Could you step on it, please?" MacKenzie cried.

I sat in the backseat with her—in serious fucking pain—while Ty drove us to the emergency room. My left eye was swelling shut and my face was bleeding in a few places, but that wasn't what worried me. My shoulder had been crushed during the fight, and now I couldn't move my arm. Which meant it was bad.

"Don't bleed on my upholstery, please," Ty said. "This is a new car."

MacKenzie wiped at my face with a sterile pad. It was pointless since the blood was now mostly dry, but I let her do it because it seemed to calm her. Her touch was so gentle, it pulled my mind off the pain.

"We're almost there, Ian," she said.

I shouldn't have noticed it, because there was so much of my own blood all over, but as she dabbed at my face I saw several crescent-shaped wounds in her palm. I pulled her hand away from my face to get a better look.

"You're bleeding," I said. "Who did this to you?" Damn it, was this why she'd been crying earlier? Did that jerk do this to her? "Who did this?"

"It was an accident," she said and balled her hand up in mine. That was when I made the connection. She'd done it to herself. Her own nails matched up with the tiny cuts on the palm of her hand.

"What happened?" I opened her hand and held it gently in mine, lightly stroking the marks with my thumb. She blinked and a tear ran down her cheek. "Why did you do this?" I asked, and another tear fell down her cheek. "God, Kenzie, what's wrong?"

"It's allergies." She shook her head and sniffed, wiping at her eyes.

This was not fucking allergies. I couldn't stand watching a chick cry. Hell, normally I would run in the other direction, but with Kenzie it was different. I didn't want her to cry because I didn't want her to feel pain, ever.

I wrapped my good arm around her and pulled her head to my chest, then immediately wondered if she wouldn't gag at the fact that I had blood, sweat, and grime all over me from the fight. But she didn't resist, instead she surprised me by folding up closer to me. I touched my lips to the top of her head and took a deep breath. She smelled like honey and vanilla. *Damn it.* I knew she was sweet, and this was fucking killing me.

"We're here," Ty announced from the front seat, then looked back at us. His mouth dropped open, but he quickly closed it.

"C'mon," Kenzie said as she sat up. She wiped her face with her sleeve, then got out of the car without looking at me.

Eleven

What the hell was I thinking when I agreed to work with Ian on his rehab?

The truth was, I knew exactly what I was thinking. I had seen the pain in his eyes when the doctor gave him his prognosis. Six to eight weeks' recovery time meant potentially missing his first pro fight, the one Chris had lined up for him in Vegas. That fight was only seven weeks away. If he was going to get back in shape and have a shot at winning that fight, he needed all the help he could get.

Which was why I was sitting on my living room floor with Alexa at three o'clock in the morning, surrounded by every anatomy textbook I had, laptops open. As a nurse, I knew anatomy. But to get him through the injury, I needed to brush up on some of the physical therapy aspects. Lucky for me, she had offered to help.

Alexa worked night shifts at the hospital, so she was used to being up this late, but I never stayed up late unless I was out at a club and being highly entertained. So, almost never. To compensate, I was pounding my fifth cup of coffee.

I gave her a sly smile. "You don't need to stay up this late. It's your night off, go bang your hot-ass boyfriend. At least then one of us will be getting laid tonight."

Alexa laughed and blushed, but then she got a far-off look in her eyes. "I'm sure I can stay a bit longer with you and still manage to get laid." She paused, then said, "What's going on with you and Ian, anyway?"

She looked a little wary, as if I might bite her for asking, which was weird because I always talked to her about guys. But as I tried to answer the question, I realized Ian was different. I felt something for him deep inside, in a place I *never* shared, not with anyone.

"Nothing's going on," I insisted. "I'm dating Chris." *I think.* "I'm just helping Ian recover."

She gave me that look she always did when she knew I was lying, but wasn't sure she should call me on it.

I sighed. "What?"

"It's just that you seemed so upset that Ian got hurt, and then there was the night you called me from dinner. What did you call him that night? Amazing?"

"So? I was drunk. Everyone's amazing when I'm drunk."

It was kind of true, but I felt my fingers dig into my palms again. Alexa needed to back off or I'd break. *Please don't let me fall apart again.*

"Oh, okay," she said.

This time when she gave me her Kenzie-you're-so-full-of-it look, I just ignored it. That was how she knew not to push anymore. Alexa was an expert at reading people and knowing when not to push, something I absolutely valued in a friend.

I turned back to the book I was reading, only I could hardly concentrate on the words in front of me. My thoughts kept returning to the moment in Ty's car when Ian had pulled me close and just held me. Why did he do that? Why was he so pushy, trying to find out why my hands were bleeding? No one ever cared about that, so why did he?

God, I felt like such an idiot for falling apart in front of him, but in that moment, it just felt so good to let him hold me. It was like his strong embrace held me together.

I'd never fallen apart like that before. I hated it. Something about Ian was just so protective and so safe that for just a moment I felt like it was okay to let go. I hated that he did that to me because I don't let go. I don't cry in front of other people. Ever. It makes you vulnerable, and when you're vulnerable, people can hurt you.

And honestly, what was I even crying about? The fight before Ian's, I was eating it up—the competition, the testosterone filling the room. Hell, I even loved it when Ian was messing with Steel. But when Steel punched Ian in the throat and I saw the very real pain in Ian's eyes, how he fought for breath, something changed. I raced for the cage, wanting— no, *needing*—to make sure he was okay.

When I realized I was holding my breath, I knew. I needed him to breathe in the same way I needed my own breath. It was so stupid. So weak.

"There's nothing going on between us, not at all," I told Alexa. And at that moment, I was determined that I would mean it. But the thought of spending so much one-on-one time with him during his recovery made my chest tighten, and I knew I was in trouble.

Twelve

Ian's address told me that his place had to be nice; I just didn't realize how luxurious it would be. I couldn't help compare his building to mine. My ugly little four-story was a reality-cop-show backdrop, whereas his was closer to the set of the next rich playboy movie. His building was about a hundred years older than mine, yet in much better shape. It was beautiful.

I was craning my neck to appreciate the detailed architecture about twenty stories up when a doorman opened the door for me. He checked to make sure my name was on the list before motioning for me to go past the desk. "Down the hall, take a left, last one at the end."

At least Ian lived on the first floor. I didn't think I could handle it if he'd lived in a fancy top-floor penthouse. My tennis shoes squeaked on the marble floors as I followed the doorman's directions.

I was wearing what I always wore to the gym, having just come from there, but here my short-shorts and tank top felt ridiculously inadequate. I wrapped my arms around myself to stay warm in the air-conditioning, and maybe also to cover up a little since I was starting to nip out. As I made my way down the hall, I wondered if I would be able to coach him through physical therapy with my arms locked across my chest. *Yeah, right.* He'd just better not give me crap about it or I was leaving.

I found the last door, and Ian opened it before I had a chance to knock.

"Hey…" I had a billionaire joke on the tip of my tongue, but when I saw him, the playful smirk on my face fell. It had been over a week since the fight, but his eye still bore the dark marks of bruising, and the gash over his eyebrow they'd stitched up in the ER hadn't healed yet. I instinctively stepped forward, wanting to brush away the pain I saw there, but I held myself back. This was a professional visit. I was here to help Ian work on his injury.

There was nothing going on between us. He knew it. I knew it.

He wore loose shorts and a clean white T-shirt. His left arm was immobilized, strapped to his chest with a complex brace. He hadn't worked out in over a week—doctor's orders—and yet his arm muscles still bulged as if he could rip out of the brace's straps at any moment. It made the contraption look like some sort of joke.

"I hadn't knocked yet," I stammered.

"The doorman called to let me know you were here." As he spoke, I realized I was looking down at his firm calf muscles. I forced my gaze back up his body to meet his eyes. They were soft—for him—and he looked sleepy.

"Must be nice to have a doorman," I said. "Did I wake you?"

He rubbed his free hand over his short hair. "Actually, I did sleep in a bit today."

He stepped back to let me in. As I walked past, I caught a hint of his scent—soapy with a hint of musk. Of course he smelled amazing.

Just business, I reminded myself. This visit was going to be tricky.

The room was not what I'd expected, since it obviously wasn't his apartment. Instead it was a small gym with several types of punching bags, a mat, free weights, and all the machines he needed to work out.

"If your building has such nice facilities, why do you even go to the gym?"

"This isn't the building's facility." He paused and smiled a little. "I rent this unit. This is my own personal gym. If I kept all this in my condo, my downstairs neighbor would shoot me. I live upstairs in a different unit."

I made a mental note that he might be a little more well off than I thought. The billionaire jokes threatened to resurface, but I held back. "Okay, so why do you even bother with Chris's gym?"

"Here I don't have sparring partners or coaches."

"Right. Of course."

I pulled my bag off my shoulder and looked around for a good place to stash it. He took it from me, his hand brushing against mine as he did. Just that small touch sent my nerves singing and gave me goose bumps.

Ian set my bag on a chair by the door, then turned back to me. His eyes smoldered. Was it possible to be caressed with only a look? His Adam's apple moved as he swallowed, then he reached to the wall behind me, grabbed a hoodie from a hook, and held it up in front of me.

"You're cold." His gaze drifted down almost imperceptibly.

Damn it, I was still nipping out. This was going great.

I pulled on the sweatshirt, even though the sun coming in through the windows made the place warm. My nipples weren't exactly reacting to the cold anymore, but he didn't need to know that.

"Let's get you out of that brace." I stepped toward him and reached out, but he took a step back.

"I've got it," he said. He managed to open the first Velcro strap, but he struggled with the next.

"Just let me help you, or we'll be here all day."

I closed the gap between us before he could retreat again, and gently pulled his free arm from its impossible task. Holding his shoulder in place with one hand, I slowly pulled open the brace to release his arm.

"How the heck have you been managing with this thing all by yourself for the last week?" As I asked, I realized I had no idea if he'd been alone for the last week. Maybe he'd had his new adult-movie-star girlfriend, "the screamer," taking care of him.

Not that it was any of my business. So why was I searching his eyes for any hint that he might not have been alone? But he remained silent, quietly studying me. God, I was making myself sick. Why couldn't I just let it go?

"Let's start by testing your strength," I said. "Put your hand on my shoulder."

Ian smiled and effortlessly raised his right arm. His hand gently cupped my shoulder. I was thankful that I was wearing his sweatshirt, because his touch was doing crazy things to me.

I took a breath and said, "Other hand, genius," giving him an exaggerated eye roll.

His nostrils flared and his eyes widened at the effort, but he couldn't manage to get his arm much higher than his waist. His hand shook and he let out a grunt before dropping his arm, swearing under his breath. "Shit."

"I guess we have our work cut out for us," I said.

"We? I appear to be the only one breaking a sweat here."

"Yes. We." I stepped closer and helped him lift his hand, placing it on my shoulder. His arm, being all muscle, was heavier than it looked, and as soon as I rested it on my shoulder, he took another step closer and tightened his grip.

"Am I hurting you?" he asked.

"No," I said. "Push down."

I waited but felt nothing, no push from his hand. But with him so close, I felt a push of a different nature that needed to be nipped in the bud. And there was only one way for me to stop this growing desire before it got totally out of control.

"How's Sara?"

Thirteen

Of course I knew it was a bad idea for MacKenzie to come over and help out with physical therapy at my place. I'm an MMA fighter, not a fucking moron. Still, I felt like one for suggesting it.

I didn't know if she felt the same way or not, but she agreed to come over. Which was good because I wasn't ready to go back to the gym. I didn't need the guys watching me while I struggled to lift my hand any higher than my waist.

But I had no clue how to act with her now. She'd let me hold her in Ty's car on the way to the ER, and it seemed so right, but then as soon as we got to the hospital, she pulled away and acted like it never happened. So the only way I could figure to deal, was the same way she was dealing with it. Or not dealing with it.

Shit, women should come with manuals. She was lucky she was so amazing.

MacKenzie came over wearing her usual gym clothes, including my favorite pair of short-shorts— so short I could see a crescent of the naked curve of her fabulous ass whenever she bent over. On top she wore a low-cut tank that hugged the curves of her slender waist and clung tight to her exceptional breasts. Her nipples were erect, which made it impossible to not imagine her naked. It was going to be a hard fucking workout. At least I managed to get her to put on a sweatshirt.

Even as she jabbed at me verbally, I couldn't help noticing her gentle nature as she helped me out of my brace. And when she stepped closer and put my hand on her shoulder, her tiny little frame in my huge hand made me want to say, fuck it. Just take control of the situation and pull her the rest of the way to me. God, I wanted to kiss her—and do a lot more to her—so fucking bad.

"How's Sara?" she asked.

The words startled me. Where the fuck did they come from? I thought I detected a hint of a smirk. *Fuck.* I turned away from her to give myself a second. Why wouldn't the Sara thing just die already? I considered keeping up the charade and telling her we were still dating, but I just wanted to be done with the whole mess.

"I'm not sure, to be honest," I said and added, "That was our first and last date," hoping that would put an end to the whole topic.

But the hint of a smirk resurfaced on MacKenzie's face. Double fucking shit. Here we go…jokes about one-night stands, maybe?

"So I guess porn stars are good enough to have as friends, and good for one-night stands, but not dating material?"

Triple fucking shit. How did she know about Sara's adult film work? Of course she did. She was MacKenzie. I bet she watched Cade's films.

Her face was so smug, I wanted to kiss that smirk right off her face. Because even when she was being a little brat, it still all came back to that. I imagined nibbling on her pouty lower lip as I considered how much more I wanted her to know. If in fact there was anything left she didn't know. God, I hoped she didn't know I paid Sara. But Cade would never betray me like that.

"We didn't sleep together," I said.

Her smile faded and her eyes widened. "So, it's true then?"

My breathing stopped. She *did* know I paid for Sara to accompany me. I would be kicking Cade's ass the next time I saw him.

"What's true?" I asked cautiously. I might have paid for a night with a porn star, but I wasn't going to admit to it that easily.

"That you don't have sex before a big fight." Her look was so innocent and hopeful, yet it still took me a second to figure out why she was asking this.

"Yes," I finally answered. Her cute little frame seemed to relax a little, making me feel—once again—like a total dick. She didn't know I paid Sara; she was talking about something completely different, about the night we almost hooked up. The night I told her I couldn't because I had a fight the next day.

She chewed at the inside of her cheek a moment, maybe considering what I'd just said. Shit, that meant she thought I'd just made that up to get rid of her. Not fucking likely. Putting the brakes on that night had been the hardest thing I'd ever done.

"So," she said as she looked up at me innocently through her eyelashes. "What does that do? For a fighter, I mean."

I chuckled. "You mean besides frustrate the hell out of us?"

She smiled—thank fucking goodness—then nodded for me to continue.

"You know that stereotype that most guys are boneheaded cave dwellers driven by instinct?"

"Is it considered a stereotype if it's true?" she said, then giggled.

God, she had a great laugh.

I nodded. "That's what I was getting at. On some very basic level, we fight in order to survive and procreate."

She scrunched up her nose, making her look super cute. "But wouldn't you fight better then? If you have sex, then you have someone to fight for, right?"

Her hand went up to mine, which was still resting on her shoulder. She absentmindedly played with my fingers until she noticed I was watching her, and realized what she'd been doing. She let her hand drop.

I shook my head. "We fight to procreate. Once we've had sex, we've done the job and have no reason to fight."

"Hmm." She nodded. "So I guess now that you aren't fighting for a while, you're free to take care of business." Her gaze drifted down my body.

My dick screamed at me to pull her close. She was stating the obvious, but it felt like she was suggesting more. I saw the hunger in her eyes.

Fuck. Did she know what she was doing to me? If I thought I was any ounce of good enough for her, I'd show her how I *take care of business.*

I took a deep breath. There was no way I could be reading her right; after all, she was dating Chris. I needed to back off.

"Yeah," I said. "With my arm all messed up, I'm not planning any big rendezvous anytime soon."

MacKenzie took a deep breath. "Right, so let's start on your stretches."

Fourteen

MACKENZIE

The deal was that I would spend two hours a day twice a week with Ian, working on his physical therapy exercises and stretches. And apparently that was *all* he wanted to work on.

I couldn't believe I'd flat-out asked him why he didn't have sex before a fight. So much for being "professional." I hated what happened after that, though. I'd basically baited him by reminding him he didn't have an upcoming fight, and he still wouldn't go near me.

So that was it. I was done throwing myself at him. In fact, if I wasn't behind in rent, I might have even quit. But I still needed the job, so I would make the best of it.

The new guy Chris brought in to train with Ian arrived at the gym the next morning. Evidently he didn't get the memo that Ian was temporarily benched. The new guy's name was Jonah, which made me laugh, because he seriously was the size of a freaking whale. He kept himself busy by coaching the other guys at the gym on what they called "ground and pound," which also made me laugh. Who in the world thought that was a good fighting term?

Jonah didn't bother taking it easy on the guys, which kept me busy. I was working on one of his latest victims when Chris called me into his office. I put a Band-Aid on a guy's chin, which had already stopped bleeding, then assured him that he didn't need stitches before following Chris to see what he needed.

"What's up, boss?" I asked as he took a seat at his desk. I sat down on the couch across from him. He'd surprised me by actually managing to keep it all business at work. Maybe not all guys were cavemen.

"I just wanted to check how things were going with you."

"Fine," I said. "Jonah's keeping me busy."

He laughed, then leaned forward, folding his arms on his desk. "How are things with Ian? The little twerp has been refusing to go to the doctor to get a checkup, so while he's out of the gym, you're my only source." He winked.

The fact that Ian was refusing to go to the doctor was news to me. I would have to get on him for that. We'd only just started working together one-on-one.

"He's doing okay," I said. "I would like to see him improve a little faster, but he'll get there." *I hope.*

Chris nodded. "Good. I don't want to see him miss out on his first big fight." He leaned back in his chair and opened a drawer, pulling out an envelope. "I know this is early, but I was writing out the payroll checks today, so I figured I might as well give this to you now."

"Thank you." I reached out and took the envelope. He had no idea how close I'd been to asking for an advance on my paycheck. This would be just enough to get my rent up-to-date. *Thank God.*

He pushed up from the desk and sauntered over to the couch, taking a seat next to me. "So, MacKenzie, can we pretend we aren't at work long enough for me to ask you to dinner tonight?" He took my hand in his and wove his fingers through mine.

Chris was sweet sometimes. I had been warming up to him, but still wanted to take it slow. He seemed eager to move forward to the next level, whatever that was, but I wasn't ready yet. Thank God he'd been patient with me.

"I have girls' night tonight, remember?"

He gave me a big smile. "I do, but I was hoping it was canceled or something. A guy can dream, right?" He kissed the back of my hand. "We're still on for Friday night, though, aren't we?"

"Yeah." He'd begun to refer to Friday as our "date night," a phrase that for some reason had my stomach twisting in knots. But I tried not to think about it.

Fifteen

The first one-on-one session with MacKenzie had nearly killed me. Not because of the pain—I could handle that—but having her bounce around me in that low-cut tank top was torture. I had to use every trick I knew to keep my dick from giving her a constant personal salute.

I decided today would be different, which was why I took an extra-long shower before our next appointment, soaping myself up to take care of business. I would never make it through another session with her without a release.

All I had to do was think of her—her round ass, her heavy tits, or her long, slender legs—and I got hard. It was always her. I'd tried thinking about other women, but I always came back to MacKenzie.

We hadn't gone very far that night she still hated me for, but I hadn't forgotten the sweet taste of her soft mouth. I imagined it sucking my cock as I stroked it, her skillful tongue and lips massaging my shaft. It was hardly any time before I was brought to the edge.

As I came, I imagined all the ways I wanted her—riding me on the bench in my gym, against the wall just out of sight of the window, or finishing what we started in the back of my car. Most of all, I wanted to have her in my bed. I imagined thrusting into her hot, wet cunt with her tight little ass in the air, and I came so fucking hard.

****

Downstairs in the gym, MacKenzie helped me through each of the exercises. This time I could actually concentrate on the different stretches and movements—for the most part.

"Here, let me show you again," she said.

We were on my final round of reps, and she was still amazingly patient as she showed me the same exercise for the millionth time. She took the stretch band from my grasp and stepped between me and the wall.

I'd gotten rid of my shirt because it was restricting my movements, and now her warm shoulder blades and the tickle of her hair brushed against my bare chest. She lifted my hand, putting it on her shoulder so I could feel which muscles she was working.

"Pull back like this, see, and—" Her voice cut off.

That was when I realized I'd been holding her body to mine, my hand splayed across her abdomen in a possessive gesture. I looked down, wondering if she would look up at me with her beautiful eyes full of want or confusion, but she only stood there silently, neither leaning into me nor pulling away.

"Sorry," I grunted. I channeled every ounce of self-restraint I had and released her, taking one step back.

She took a deep breath and began again, almost as if nothing had happened. "Just pull back like this, engaging this muscle here."

Without looking at me, she placed her free hand over mine on her shoulder. Damn, her touch was so gentle. She moved my hand over the soft skin of her shoulder until she found the muscle she was talking about. She was strong, even as small as she was.

I focused on the movement as she pulled the band tight, and then released. Then it was my turn again. I mimicked her movements through the last round of reps, and she started packing up to leave.

"Where did you park?" I asked. "I forgot to tell you, you can use the garage when you're here. I have a guest pass."

She shook her head. "That's okay, I ride the bus. I don't own a car."

"Oh." I was dumbfounded. How had I not known that? "I'll drive you home then." I pulled my shirt back on and grabbed my keys. There was no way I was going to let her take the bus home.

"No, it's fine. I take the bus all the time," she said.

"Not anymore, you don't."

She smiled coyly. "Are you volunteering to be my personal chauffeur?"

"No, but you leave here late enough that some of the weirdos have already started to come out. The least I can do is give you a ride home."

She didn't say anything at first, running her hand through her hair. "Fine."

She sounded almost like it was painful to accept help from me. I didn't know if she was that way with everyone, or if I should take it personally. But it didn't matter, because I would be driving her home.

MacKenzie didn't talk much on the way to her place other than to give me directions, which left me to wonder if she was upset about me pressing up against her.

As we drove, I became aware that Kenzie was directing me toward one of the worst parts of town. At first, I was hopeful that we were just passing through, but at every turn, we drove farther and farther in, until finally she asked me to stop in front of a building I wouldn't have guessed was hers in a million years. It might have passed building inspections, having all its windows and such, but that was about all I could say for the place. It was one of those block apartment buildings from the seventies. All the windows were filthy and had cheap twisted-up blinds.

The worst part, though, was the neighborhood. I counted several dealers and hookers on our ride here, and the sun wasn't even down yet.

"Thanks," MacKenzie said and hopped out of the car.

"Hang on, I'll walk you up." I followed her, my pulse kicking like a fucking mule. It would take every ounce of strength I had to leave her in this place. I would make damn sure the locks were secured before I left her.

"It's no big deal."

"I'd feel better knowing I got you all the way inside safely." Understatement of the goddamn year.

She shrugged and rolled her eyes at me as if I was going overboard, but she let me follow her inside.

"Do you know any self-defense moves?" I asked as I followed her up the steps.

"Thanks a lot." She laughed. "My neighborhood isn't that bad."

"So, that's a no?"

She shrugged again. "The building's secure."

"What if I teach you some moves, you know, just in case?" Or move you into a safer apartment, I added silently.

MacKenzie stopped on the steps, considering, but then continued. "It's okay, you don't have to do that. I'm fine. I've been taking care of myself for years."

Damn it, why did she have to be so independent and self-reliant all the time?

"Fine," I said. But this wasn't over. Maybe I could work with Chris to get her a raise so she didn't have to live here. If I had to pay the difference myself, so be it. It would be worth it to be able to sleep at night and not worry about her.

She stopped in front of her door and turned to me. "Thanks. Again. I think I've got it from here."

But something was off. "Hang on," I said, holding her there. "I heard yelling."

She giggled. "It's just the kids on the street, calm down."

But then we heard more yelling. It was coming from her neighbor's apartment, just next door. I pushed MacKenzie behind me as the shouts grew louder. Glass shattered, and it sounded like someone was throwing pots and pans.

"Soni," MacKenzie shrieked, and I felt her small hands cling to the back of my shirt.

The door burst open and a teenage boy rushed out of the apartment with a wild look in his eyes. I pushed MacKenzie farther back, holding out my good arm in case he wanted to attack. His eyes were wild as he glanced around for a way out, but we were in his path.

Fuck, I was going to have to take him down.

"No, Ian!" MacKenzie cried after me as I went to meet him head-on.

"Call the police," I growled as I grabbed the kid's hand, twisting it. He flipped immediately, as I knew he would, but he had to be tweaking on something, because he managed to bounce to his feet and pull himself free. "Shit," I grumbled.

I went at him again, first kicking him in the side to destabilize him, then bringing him down again. This time I held him around the neck so that his airflow was cut off. Still, he continued to kick around frantically like a fish out of water.

"Calm the fuck down," I said, lifting him up and slamming his butt on the ground for emphasis. He wouldn't get hurt if he would just stop resisting.

"The police are on their way," MacKenzie said as she tucked her phone back into her bag.

The guy wouldn't give up, so I twisted his arm back, forcing him onto his stomach, and sat on him.

When MacKenzie saw I had the kid immobilized, she darted past us into her neighbor's place.

Shit. "You better be alone," I growled at the little shit who'd become my new chair. "Are you alone?" I could hold this guy back with only one arm, but if there were more of them, we were in trouble.

"Just me," he managed to wheeze out. "Please let me go. I promise, you'll never see me again."

I ignored him, letting the stupid kid whine, which he continued to do like a fucking pussy.

As I waited for the police, I started to worry about MacKenzie. There were no noises coming from the apartment at all, which worried the shit out of me. I was about to leave the kid on the ground and go in after her when the police finally showed up, and I was able to run in and check on her.

Sixteen

At first when Ian said he wanted to give me self-defense lessons, I thought he was kidding. I should have known he wouldn't joke about that kind of thing. Even after what happened the other night, I maintained that my neighborhood wasn't that bad. The kid Ian tackled was Soni's grandson. He came over and asked her for money every once in a while. Admittedly, that night he was worse than usual, but I still knew how to call 911.

Unfortunately, that wasn't enough for Ian. As far as he was concerned, the situation only illustrated his point. Which was why I was in Ian's personal gym, about to get my first lesson in self-defense. That, and I told him I'd do it if he agreed to go back to the doctor for his two-week checkup.

"So," I said. "What do you think you can teach me with only one arm?"

"You saw what I did to that kid in your building the other night, right?" His lips tugged up in a playful smirk.

As much as I didn't want to be affected by Ian, I loved this side of him. His protective nature made my belly clench. And coupled with his confidence and that spark of boyish charm? I might as well hand over my panties now.

"Or do I need to show you again?" He stepped forward quickly, and I instinctively held my hands up, turning to run. "Good." He stopped.

"Good, what?" I turned back to him.

"That was your first lesson. Any situation where you feel you're in danger, if you can, run."

"Okay." That I knew how to do. And it seemed pretty obvious.

"Lesson number two. If you can't run, go for the eyes."

"I know that one," I said. "Because they're always guarding their family jewels first, and won't expect that."

"Right. I thought you said you didn't know any self-defense."

I shrugged. "This is all just common street knowledge. Ears and nose are good targets too. If you want to teach me something new, teach me how to break out of a hold or disable an attacker."

"Okay, sure. Lesson number three. How to break out of a hold." He stepped forward and his cool eyes on mine felt almost predatory, but I didn't step back, holding my ground. He slid his arm around my waist.

I put my hands up on his chest, pushing him back. "Wait. Maybe we should hold off on these classes until your shoulder's healed. I don't want to make it worse."

Ian didn't answer, instead sweeping my feet out from under me. He lay me down on the mat and covered me, hovering inches above me between my legs. My heart raced from the thrill of being thrown down so effortlessly and yet so gently.

His lips turned up into a smug grin. "Don't worry. I've got it under control."

My God, if he could do all that with just one arm, what would it be like to work with him at full strength? The thought aroused me, making me even more aware of how close he was to my center. All he had to do was let gravity take his body down, and I would feel him between my legs. As it was, my body ached to rise up and press against his, just inches away.

"What now?" I asked, my voice coming out softer than I'd intended.

His jaw clenched and he waited a moment, just staring at me. If I didn't know better, I would have thought he was about to kiss me.

I scanned his face, noting his chin was rough with stubble, which I imagined would feel rough against my cheeks. Lying there with Ian between my legs, I was so flustered I almost pulled him to me right then.

"Try to get up," he said.

I laughed. Pretending for a moment that I actually wanted to get up from my current position, there was no way in hell I would be able to overpower Ian.

"Just try."

So I did, halfheartedly at first, but once I really started getting into it, I managed to twist myself around so that I was on my stomach. He was still on top of me and still had my legs spread, only now he was pressing his body against mine as I tried to resist. I wiggled my ass against his pelvis and heard him release a grunt. My pulse kicked up a notch as I shuddered at that sensual sound coming from him.

I twisted around again. No matter how careful he was to keep our groin areas apart, my attempts to free myself had me constantly rubbing up against him in a way that should have felt wrong, but felt so very right. At one point, his leg pressed firmly against my pubic bone, and the throbbing was immediate and delicious. I pushed myself into him without even thinking, just wanting some release. I must have stopped struggling because he relaxed his grip, and after a beat, pulled his leg away.

"What the fuck, Kenzie?" His eyes found mine. He rolled off me, looking a little winded.

"What?"

"You're not even trying."

Thankful that he didn't chastise me for seeking friction against him, I kept quiet. We were silent for a few tense seconds, and I wondered if he could hear the dull roar of my pulse thrumming in my neck, or see the desire that had to be written all over my flushed face.

"You take the offensive pose, and I'll show you some ways to get out of a hold like that."

I nodded, thankful the tense moment had passed. Now I just needed to find a way to survive the remainder of these lessons without dry humping his leg.

Seventeen

Alexa grabbed my drink so that I could carry the shots back to our table where Ty, the dutiful designated driver, was sipping a soda. I'd already had a few drinks, so walking was becoming a bit of an adventure.

"I don't understand why you made us come here," Alexa said. "Usually girls' night is a quiet bar these days. Are we celebrating something?"

I shook my head. "Can't a girl just want to go out dancing with her friends every once in a while? We used to come here all the time. When did nightclubs become criminal activity warranting the third degree?"

She rolled her eyes at me, and we scooted back into our seats.

"Are you guys ready to leave yet?" Ty asked when we sat down.

I laughed. "When did you guys get so old? We just got here. At least let me get a good buzz and a dance in." I pushed one of the kamikazes in front of Alexa, and we toasted. "To girls' night." I downed mine and chased it with beer.

"I'm just saying," Ty said. "We could have at least gone to the Rainbow Room."

"We went there last month," I reminded him. "Besides, it's a lot easier for me to pick up straight men." I slapped my hand over my mouth, but it couldn't put the words back in.

Alexa's eyes got wide and Ty's jaw dropped.

"What?" I said. "It's been a while. I just want to get laid." It was my standard stock answer, but for some reason tonight it didn't feel right.

"Don't you have a boyfriend?" Ty asked.

"I don't know." I shrugged. "Chris and I haven't slept together yet, it's not official."

Ty put his hand up as if to stop me. "Isn't that part of the reason you have a boyfriend? That's one of the benefits, right? That you have a warm, willing body when you need it?"

I knew they wouldn't understand, which was why I hadn't planned on telling them I wanted to get laid tonight. Hell, I was so confused, I hardly understood myself. As I sat there, under their watchful, worried stares, it struck me that this is exactly what the old me would have done. I was feeling sorry for myself, and whenever that happened, I threw myself at the first cute man I saw, drinking and dancing, and maybe more to try and make myself feel better. But a dozen years of the same broken cycle should have taught me that it never actually works that way.

Ian and I had gone over self-defense scenarios all afternoon. It turned out he was a really good teacher, and by the end of the day, I could get out from under him without too much effort. But in the course of my lesson, he'd spent enough time between my legs that I really needed a release. But I couldn't go to Chris for that. Because once we crossed that bridge, there was no going back.

"So, what's going on with you and Chris?" Alexa asked, pulling me from my thoughts.

"I'm not sure we're ready to go to the next level yet," I said.

Alexa leaned forward. "You mean, *you* aren't ready. I seriously doubt he has any inhibitions."

I shrugged and took a swig of my beer. The last shot was hitting me harder than the others, and things were starting to spin a little. *Crap.*

"I didn't want to say anything," Alexa said. "Because I was so glad you were finally dating someone, but are you being fair to Chris? After all, you obviously like…" She paused. "Well, you don't seem to like Chris that much. And…" She put her fist down on the table. "Fuck it, I'll say it. You still like

Ian. You don't have to date Ian, but it's not fair that you lead Chris around when you like someone else."

I flinched. Alexa had never barked like that at me before.

I pushed myself up to my feet and said, "You don't know anything." Then the room spun, and I fell back into my chair. "Shit. I can't date Ian anyway. He doesn't want me. But I like Chris. We kiss."

Chris and I had kissed a few times since we started dating, yet I still wasn't sure I even wanted to be dating him. One thing was for sure—Alexa's nagging wasn't helping me figure it out.

Ty reached across the table and put his hand on mine. "She's right, you know." He leaned in. "I was at the last fight. I saw how you were with Chris. He jumped in to save you from that guy who was bugging you, and you barely said thank you to him before you ran back to sit next to me, and your eyes were on Ian the entire time."

"So? Was I supposed to be all, 'Oh, my hero!'? I'm not like that. I can take care of myself."

Ty's eyes widened. "Are you listening to yourself right now? You are so full of shit. That whole evening, you had been telling me how you liked to pretend the fighters were fighting for your honor." He lifted his hand as if to wave me off.

I responded by waving him off too, but didn't say a word. Damn, I had to be drunk. Usually I had a comeback for this kind of stuff.

"Whatever, MacKenzie. And then there was the way you kept on flying to the cage anytime Ian was hit."

"That's my job," I said. God, what the hell was this, an intervention?

"What about the ride to the ER? What was that in the back of my car? I saw him holding you. Damn, y'all are both idiots."

They might be right, I did like Ian, but so what, he would never be mine, and I still thought I could make things work with Chris. Maybe. "Can we please talk about something else?" I said, flagging down a waitress and ordering another round of shots.

Ty and Alexa shared a look, then relaxed a little, leaning back in their seats. I breathed a sigh of relief, knowing that their prying was over, for now anyway.

I abandoned any thoughts of getting laid, realizing that wasn't what I wanted or needed. As for what I did want, I had no idea, so I tried not to think about it, instead throwing back a few more shots than I should have, forcing us to leave before the club even got busy.

On the way home I passed out in the back seat.

When I woke up, we were parking in front of Alexa's house. She and Ty helped me inside and set me on the sofa.

"Alexa, I'm really sorry about tonight. You guys are right, Ian is totally flipping awesome. He's hot, right? But he's also so sweet. Did you know he's teaching me self-defense?"

Alexa smiled. "Get some rest." She pulled a blanket up over me, and I was out again.

Eighteen

IAN

It felt good to be back at the gym. Chris's gym, that is. I was only there to talk business with Chris, still doing all my training at the home gym, but I was going stir crazy, and it was great to see the guys again.

"Hey, gimpy," Chris said to greet me when I walked into his office.

"Hey, douche-roll." I sat down on the couch. "I see you're still running this place into the shitter."

"You didn't see the new talent when you came in?" he asked.

I assumed he was talking about the guy who was making meatloaf out of one of the guys in the practice cage. "Where did you find him?"

"That's Jonah. He's the guy I brought in to train with you."

"Yeah, uh, I don't know if you noticed, but I can't really fight right now." I pointed at the arm strapped to my chest in a brace.

"He was looking for a new gym and excited about moving to the city, so I told him to come anyway. He's integrated into the family quite well."

"What is he, welterweight?" I asked.

Chris shook his head. "Nope, he's middleweight, just like you. He's already had several pro fights. You need to hurry up and get yourself back together so you can try him out."

"We're working on it." I looked out through the one-way glass to the gym's treadmill. It was empty.

"She doesn't work today."

"Huh?" I turned back to him. "Yeah, I know. How are things going with you two?" I hadn't meant to ask, but when it came to MacKenzie, I couldn't help myself. I had to know.

He nodded. "All good. I'm thinking about asking her to come with us to Vegas for the fight. Obviously it would be good to have her there to help you with your last-minute training, but I also thought it would be nice to stay after with her and do a long weekend."

Fuck. That was what I got for asking. Now I couldn't find my stupid words. And to make it worse, I think my mouth might have been hanging open.

"What? You think it's too soon?"

I shrugged, then shook my head. "I don't know, dude. I'm not dating her, you are. Have you asked her yet?"

"No, I was hoping to ask her this Friday. I have a big date planned, and I thought that would be the big reveal at the end."

I hated this conversation. I knew I needed to stay out of MacKenzie's love life, but that didn't mean I wanted to hear about other people enjoying her.

Thankfully my phone buzzed. I dug it out of my pocket. It was Sophia.

"Hey, Sis. Where the hell have you been?" I got up and motioned to Chris that I had to take the call, and stepped out of the office.

"Hi, Ian." Her voice sounded overly casual. "I've been busy. Sorry I haven't called you back. Look, I need a little help…do you think you could loan me some money?"

I sighed. Sophia was lousy with money. We both got the same monthly amount from our trust funds, but she always managed to burn through hers in the first three weeks. We'd just gotten our money for the month last week, though. This was early for her.

"Did you ask Mom and Dad?" I asked, knowing full well that she hadn't. They were trying to teach her fiscal responsibility, which meant they refused to give her any more than her normal monthly amount.

"You know I can't," she said. "Come on, just a little to help me through to next month?"

"That's what you always say, Sophia. Besides, don't you still owe me like two grand from last month?" It was true, but I didn't really care. I was just messing with her.

"Ian," she whined.

Damn, I hated when she whined. "Fine. I'll loan you the money. When do you need it?"

"Is now a bad time?"

I looked back through the door to Chris's office where he sat waiting for me to finish the call. If I left now, I wouldn't have to hear him talking about MacKenzie anymore.

"I'll be over in five." I hung up and popped back into the office. "Chris, I have to run. My sister's in one of her financial holes, and I need to go dig her out."

Chris laughed. "Sure. We can talk about the plane tickets and stuff later. Call me."

The gym wasn't too far from my place, which was on the way to Sophia's. I stopped off and grabbed my checkbook, which read like the story of how often Sophia had to be bailed out. Not that I cared. I had enough to go around, but it had been getting noticeably worse lately.

I flipped through my checkbook as I rode the elevator up to her place. *Shit.* Maybe our parents were right to cut her off. Of course, that was easy for them to do since they were off sailing in the Mediterranean. Call it big-brother obligation, but I found it harder to just turn my cheek when she needed me.

When I got to the door, it took her over a minute to answer. I was beginning to wonder if I needed to go home and grab my spare key to her place, but she finally opened up and stepped out into the hallway, barring me from coming in.

"Sorry, the place is a mess," she said. "I don't want anyone to see it."

"Whatever." I shrugged. This was definitely the last check I gave her. For a while, anyway. "How much do you need?"

"Five," she said.

"I hope you mean five hundred, because if you need five thousand, you're going to have to go to a bank. I can't keep on giving you huge chunks of money."

"This is the last time, I promise. I just had car trouble and I don't have enough room on my card, so…"

I swear, she always had car trouble. For a fancy foreign car, it was in the shop an awful lot. I couldn't remember the last time I'd actually seen her driving it.

I opened the checkbook and started writing. "This is the last one, Sophia."

"Yeah, you already said that."

"I mean it, though. You're sweet and smart and a great sister, but you are also the stupidest person I know when it comes to money." I signed the check and handed it to her.

"Fine, whatever," she said as she took the check. "Is the lecture done? Because I have a date."

"The lecture is done. Is your date paying tonight, or am I?" I smiled at her. She might be a little snot, but she was also my sister. It was hard to stay mad at her.

"He is, of course. Now let me go so I can get ready."

Nineteen

One of the best things about being injured was that I could drink again. Sure, I was working out, but my arm needed to get a little better before I could go back into full training mode. So training-mode rules didn't apply.

Since I couldn't spar with Cade, we had taken to going to the bar on Fridays instead. This Friday we were out at Buddie's, a dive over in his part of town. They had a great selection of microbrews, and we were working on trying out as many as we could and still stand.

Our waitress came over to the booth and dropped off round number four, smiling at us before making her way back to the bar. It was a slow night at Buddie's.

As soon as she left, the look on Cade's face changed. I'd seen something in his expression earlier.

It was that look he got when he wanted to have one of his pussy-ass "girl talks"; that was what I called it when he wanted to get all emotional with me. The look meant he had something on his mind, and when we were drunk enough, we'd hash it out.

I pounded half my pint of beer and braced myself. "Out with it, Cade."

He took another pull from his beer, taking his time with it, then finally put the glass down on the table. "What's going on with you and MacKenzie?"

"Fuck, dude." I looked around the half-empty bar, hoping to find an easy way to get out of having this conversation. "Nothing."

"That's bullshit and you know it."

"Fuck that. I haven't slept with her. Hell, I haven't even kissed her since that night."

I was getting worked up. Cade had been the one to warn me that Kenzie had a tough upbringing, growing up in foster care, and she'd been through enough. She didn't need me dicking her over. After that, he'd launched into a speech about how she was his girl's best friend...blah, blah, blah. I'd backed off, so why I was getting a fucking lecture now, I had no clue.

Cade scooted forward in his seat. "You're getting physical therapy coaching sessions from her, and giving her one-on-one self-defense lessons, and you're telling me you've never gotten any bonus contact out of the deal?"

"Nope."

"Okay. So, when's the last time you had any pussy?"

"It's been a while, I guess." I tried to remember the last time. It had been a long while. "I've been in training mode. You know I can't chase tail while I'm training."

"You are so full of it." He knocked his beer glass against mine. "You haven't been in training mode for the entire past five months. And don't even tell me you're too injured. Do the math, you idiot. You haven't bragged once about getting laid since you met MacKenzie."

"So?" I was getting seriously pissed. He needed to drop this shit.

"Okay, then why aren't you out there getting some?"

I hadn't thought about it before, but he had a point. "Damn, are you seriously trying to be my sex therapist right now?"

"Why don't you just date her, already?"

"For the fuck of fuck. Are you shitting me?" I thought I knew what it was like to see red, but I was seeing a much more vibrant shade than I'd seen in a while. He was going to feel this at our next sparring session. "You told me to back off that night," I spat.

Cade leaned back in his seat and his eyes widened. He put his hands up in front of him. "Hey, don't explode. I didn't want you to pull a one-night stand on her. She's Alexa's best friend. They're like family. How the hell did I know you were going to go all *boombox over the head* with her?"

"You told me I couldn't touch her because it would be like you trying to date Sophia. You pulled the sister card on me."

"Fine, I un-pull the sister card."

I wanted to punch him. "It's too late. She's moved on. She's with Chris now."

"Dude, maybe I shouldn't be telling you this, but she crashed on our couch last night after a particularly intense girls' night out. I shouldn't have listened, but it was hard not to. She was shouting about how awesome you were."

For a split second, I allowed myself to consider how amazing it would be if he was right, and she really did still want me. But then I laughed. "She was drunk. How can I take that seriously?"

"Whatever. I'm just saying. If you want her, you have all the information. Stop acting like a pussy and man up before you lose your chance with her. It makes me sick to see you like this, man."

I finished off my beer. The prick might be right. "Are you done playing sex therapist now?"

Cade nodded and finished his pint. "Let's get another round."

I signaled the waitress.

Twenty

Friday night was supposed to be a big date night. At least, that was what Chris said. He wouldn't tell me where we were going or anything, which made me nervous, but he ended up taking me to a great restaurant, and afterward we went to a rooftop bar and had several rounds. I was having a good time, but starting to wonder what was so special about dinner and drinks.

Chris took a sip of his drink. "So, I know we aren't supposed to talk about work when we're out, but I've been meaning to ask you how you like working for me at the gym."

I smiled. "I can't complain. After all, I get to work out for free around a bunch of sweaty half-naked guys." I paused, wondering how I'd managed to just say such a stupid thing to my boyfriend, especially since I didn't find any of the guys at the gym that attractive. God, that was something I'd say to Alexa, not my romantic interest. "Sorry, none of them are as hot as you," I said, which felt a little like lying and I wasn't sure why. But I smiled at him.

He leaned over and kissed me quickly on the lips. "I know, honey." He put his arm around me. "The reason I ask is that I have a proposal for you. It's work related, so please don't get mad, but I was thinking about the fight Ian has coming up in just over a month. I wondered if you would want to come with us to Vegas. You know, to take care of any last-minute issues he might have."

"You want to fly me to Vegas?"

Chris paused and took another sip of his drink before answering. "Yeah, and I thought we could stay a few days after and just hang out. You know, take in the sights. Do the Vegas thing."

I took a huge swig from my drink. "You mean, like an extended date?"

"Yeah, sort of. Or maybe more like a vacation for two." He sat back to get a look at me and his brow wrinkled. "You have that look on your face. What's up?"

Damn, I sucked at hiding my feelings. I struggled to find the right words to tell him. I had slept with guys before, of course, but the idea of sharing a hotel room? That tiny little space, for several days in a row, made me feel claustrophobic. I wouldn't have my escape route, and I needed an escape route. It was how I operated.

"I just…"

"It's too soon for me to ask this, isn't it?" he asked.

Chris was seriously such a good guy, the way he always let me out of stuff like this. "No, it's just I don't know if I'm ready for the overnight thing yet. Maybe we'll be ready by then, but I can't say."

"If it's just the room thing holding you back, don't worry. We can have separate rooms."

"Can I think about it?"

"We haven't made the travel arrangements yet. Just let me know in the next few weeks."

I nodded. I spent the rest of the evening half listening to one of Chris's fight stories while I mulled over the idea of going with him to Vegas. I really wanted to go; I just didn't want to give him the wrong idea. I didn't know if I could let him pay for me to go, if I knew I wasn't ready for more yet.

When he pulled up to my apartment building at the end of the night, I was still no closer to figuring out the answer.

Chris walked me to the door and leaned in for a good-night kiss. His lips were cold and wet, and he moved his tongue in a circle, the same way every time we kissed. He wrapped his arms around me and gave me one quick, tight squeeze. This was his way of hugging. He pulled back and waited for me to unlock the entry door, then got back in his car.

Turning back, I waved to him, then let the door close and started up the steps to my floor. The hallway was quiet, which made me uneasy. It happened every now and then that the simple process of walking through the halls gave me the chills.

I used to just push through it, but lately, whenever this happened, my mind would wander to Ian, wondering where he was and wishing he could be here next to me the way he was that one day. I didn't need him to protect me or anything, I was fine on my own, but it felt so much safer when he was here. He'd been driving me home for the last several weeks after our sessions, and that he cared enough to insist on walking me to my door was so sweet.

It seemed I was growing to rely on his comforting presence more than I realized.

Twenty-One

IAN

Whenever MacKenzie came over, I couldn't help but recall her first self-defense lesson—the time my leg accidentally pressed between her legs, and how she'd eagerly pushed back. It had taken me a second to realize she wasn't struggling anymore, and her core was pressed against me as though she was aching for it. That day when I'd met her eyes, there was such a hunger in them, such a need. One I hadn't seen since the night we almost hooked up.

She'd had several lessons since then, but we'd never had that same encounter again. Which was good, because I didn't think I could resist her if it happened again.

"I don't need to know how to drop people, Ian." MacKenzie put her hands on her hips as she sassed me.

God, I wanted to spank her when she was like this. The urge to palm her hot little ass rushed through me. "I didn't want to go to the doctor, but you didn't see me bitch about it."

She laughed. "No, you didn't bitch, you whined like a freaking baby the whole way there, though."

"I told you I don't like doctors."

"Whatever, just try to keep the whining down when we go back tomorrow."

I grumbled; she just had to remind me. It was only three weeks until the big fight, and I had to go back and get another check on my progress tomorrow. I'd regained almost full use of my shoulder, but the doc wanted to see me again before he cleared me to start sparring, something I desperately needed to get back into if I was going to have any chance at the fight in Vegas.

The first doctor visit hadn't been too bad; he'd just tested my shoulder's strength and told me to keep up the good work. I still didn't want to go back, though. What if the next time he wanted me to turn my head and cough or whatever? No fucking thank you.

"I'm not going back tomorrow unless you learn how to do this. Now, get your little fanny over here and pay attention. All you do is roll the assailant over your hip, then let gravity drop them to the ground."

I demonstrated, grabbing her small frame, pulling it close to me and twisting. I rolled her body over my hip, lifting both her legs off the ground. As I did this, her soft, sweet-smelling hair brushed across my face, making me want to bring her all the way to the floor, spread her legs apart, and give her what I knew she needed.

Instead, I forced myself to set her back down on her feet. It took an incredible amount of restraint on my part.

"Okay, now I'm going to come at you. Do it just like I showed you."

Kenzie nodded that she was ready and I approached her, wrapping my arms around her. I'd fully intended to not resist and let her drop me easily to the ground—I knew how to land without getting hurt. However, she was quicker than I'd anticipated, and I wasn't ready when she twisted and sent me down to the mat.

"SHIT!"

"What! Are you hurt?" She dropped down next to me. "I'm sorry. Damn it, I told you we should have waited until you were healed." She put her soft hand on my cheek, and her eyes widened in fear.

"I'm okay." I covered her hand with mine. "It's okay. I didn't mean to scare you. I just didn't expect you to drop me so fast."

I held her small hand in mine, refusing to let it drop from my face. I found her other hand, balled up in a fist at her side, and enclosed it in mine, gently working at opening it up. The last time she'd knelt over me like this, I'd turned into a dick and pushed her away. But alone with her on the mat, in the small room that was so full of her, I couldn't do that anymore. After working one-on-one with her for several weeks, I'd worn my resistance down to the bone. I couldn't push her away.

So instead, I pulled her to me. She didn't resist, landing on top of me with a surprised *oomph*. You could only run on determination and sheer adrenaline for so long. I needed pussy. A warm, wet pussy. No, more than that, I needed MacKenzie's sexy, feisty ass in my bed. I needed to feel her moving underneath me, shifting her hips closer with my every thrust, groaning my name in her raspy tone.

The realization burst through me with surprising clarity—I didn't have the willpower to stay away from her any longer.

Her gaze latched onto mine, and her chest heaved with a succession of quick breaths.

Closing one hand around the back of her neck, I guided her mouth to mine. Her eyes drifted closed and she leaned into the kiss. It was even better than I remembered. Her lips were soft, yet demanding, and followed my lead, matching every lick of my tongue against hers.

My cell phone rang in the distance, but neither of us broke the kiss. Whoever it was would have to fucking wait.

I pulled her closer and spread her legs, placing myself between her thighs the way I'd longed to be for so fucking long. I was rock hard, and I pressed my cock between her legs. She gasped but didn't move away, letting me know how much she wanted this. I cupped her ass in my hands, squeezing tight, and pushed again. She pushed back, grinding against my dick.

Fuck. I thought I was going to lose my shit right then, she was so hot.

MacKenzie sucked on my lower lip, then broke the kiss long enough to slowly kiss her way down my neck. Her hot breath and kisses blazed a trail down my body, and she pushed my shirt out of her way. When she was at the waistband of my shorts, she looked up at me with her gorgeous eyes full of longing. Christ, she was sexy.

"Ian," she whispered. "Tell me what you want."

I wanted to pull my dick out and have her suck me off right there, but at that moment I had to touch her before I went off like a damn rocket and embarrassed myself. Last time I'd walked away without a taste, and that was not fucking happening again.

I slid one hand down to caress her cheek while she looked up at me. She leaned into my hand, letting me stroke her skin with my thumb. "Can I touch you?" I asked.

"God, yes," she said softly, breathing a warm puff of breath against my belly.

"I want to make you come. I want to hear my name on your lips."

A little grunt of satisfaction rose in her throat. I hadn't even touched her yet, and she was already so worked up.

I pulled her up toward me so she was sprawled out across my body. She was dressed in her teeny-tiny shorts and a figure-hugging tank top. I assessed this all quickly, seeking the fastest route to get her naked.

"Are you sure about this, Kenz? Because God help me, once we start, I don't know if I'll be able to stop."

I was just being honest, but the way her brows pinched together had me feeling like a real jackass. I was about to reassure her, promise her I could control myself and that we'd take this at whatever pace she needed, when she opened her mouth to speak.

"Last time, you tapped out." Her voice was small, unsure.

I lifted her chin. "That's not happening again."

"You sure you can handle it?" she taunted, her smile growing.

"I know I can't, but that's never stopped me before." I smiled back. God, this felt right. Me and her.

Before she could formulate a response, my mouth was back on hers. Hot and needy sounds pushed past her lips and into my mouth. Trailing my hands from her face, down her neck and to her shoulders, I pushed the straps of her tank top off her arms, then pulled her sports bra down her chest. Breaking free from her mouth, I looked down and nearly came in my shorts.

"These are beautiful." I pressed a kiss to the top of each breast.

A little shudder passed through her body, a signal that I read as *keep going*.

I did.

Taking one nipple in my mouth, I teased her with my tongue before sucking gently, and MacKenzie released an exquisite little groan. I gave her other breast the same treatment, palming them in my hands, licking and kissing them all over. When I paused briefly to watch her, I could see her chest and neck were flushed as if the heat was crawling up her body. I loved knowing that I was the one heating her up.

I maneuvered us quickly, flipping her so that she was laid out on her back and I was kneeling between her knees.

"Nice ground work," she teased.

"It was either nail you down to the mat, or put you on your knees," I teased right back.

"I wouldn't have minded." She smiled happily.

Christ, she shouldn't say things like that. As I trailed my hands up her thighs, MacKenzie remained propped on her elbows, watching me with wide eyes. Her skin was soft and smooth, and I loved the way she trembled under my touch. I hooked my fingers into the sides of her shorts, then tugged them and her underwear down her legs. Her tennis shoes prevented me from removing the clothes completely, but I didn't care. My goal was simple. I wanted my mouth on her hot pussy, so I bent her legs at the knee and pushed them together and up onto her chest.

She released a surprised sound, but as soon as my tongue found her wet center, the whine in her throat turned to a moan of pleasure.

Fuck, yeah.

Letting the sounds of her breathy groans guide me as to what she liked, I lightly licked from top to bottom, gripping her hips in my hands so she couldn't wiggle away. Sensing she was getting restless, I sucked her clit in my mouth and was rewarded with a hand pushed into my hair as her fingers fought for purchase.

My cell phone rang again. I promised to slowly and methodically murder whoever the fuck was interrupting this.

Ignoring the phone, I continued licking her, finding a rhythm that pushed her nearly to the edge. Then I eased one finger inside her, and her hips lifted up off the floor.

"Ian..." she groaned.

"Yeah, babe?"

"That feels so good."

Damn straight it did. This was all about her, and I couldn't wait to watch her come. Flicking my tongue against her over and over, I pushed a second finger inside her tight, hot channel, and within seconds I felt her clenching down on my hand as her release started to build.

"Come for me, sexy girl." Still pumping my fingers in and out, I bit down on her clit and MacKenzie gave a little cry of pleasure, repeating my name again and again as she came. Her body clenched down on my fingers, and tremors racked her for several long moments. Her pussy felt so good around my fingers; I couldn't wait to experience what it felt like when I was deep inside her body.

Blinking open hazy eyes, her gaze found mine and she smiled. I moved over her and kissed her deeply. MacKenzie's labored breathing was a huge turn-on. I couldn't wait to feel her hands, her mouth, her tight little cunt wrapped around me.

She curled her hand around my cock and gave it a squeeze. I almost fucking came right then. I needed to be buried balls deep inside her.

Like yesterday.

"I wanna play with this," she murmured, working her hand into the front of my shorts.

"You can do any goddamn thing you like to him."

My fucking phone started ringing again.

Motherfucker!

MacKenzie lifted her head off the mat and gave me a look that said *just go answer it.*

"Sit tight, beautiful." I needed to get rid of whoever this was—or throw the phone out the goddamn window. I got up and crossed the room, adjusting my rigid cock so I could walk properly. With a muttered curse, I grabbed my phone where it sat on the floor.

Damn it. It was Sophia. It had only been a week since I gave her the check for five grand; there was no way I was going to bail her out again. Not this soon, anyway.

I declined the call and turned back to MacKenzie, who was looking at me expectantly. She was so beautiful, it almost took my breath away. Her hair was a tangled mess, and her cheeks were rosy and pink.

But now that I was on my feet, I was having second thoughts. Not about wanting her. Hell no. But as she lay there, looking at me with her big blue eyes, I knew I didn't want her *here*, like this. MacKenzie deserved more than that. There were women you threw down on the gym mat and banged just for the sake of getting off. And there were women like MacKenzie, who you hoped would be more.

MacKenzie rose to her feet, adjusted her clothes, and closed the distance between us. She traced her fingers up my abs to my chest, then slid her arms around my neck and pulled herself up. She kissed me so tenderly, then pulled herself up on me, wrapping her legs around my waist.

I easily supported her weight with my hands under her butt. She rocked up and down against me, grinding herself on my erection. My dick flexed enthusiastically in my shorts, begging me to let him come out and play. Her damp heat radiated through my shorts, threatening to short-circuit all other thoughts in my brain.

But she deserved more. I pulled back. "MacKenzie, I can't."

Her soft eyes searched mine for a moment, wondering, before they turned cold and she let herself down, dropping to her feet.

"You fucking ass." Her hands balled up in fists. "I can't believe you're pulling this shit on me again. God, I'm such an idiot."

I stood blinking stupidly as she headed for her purse that was lying on the mat across the room. She was almost to the door before I managed to pull my shit together and take charge.

"Damn it, MacKenzie, that's not what I'm doing!" I yelled a bit too loud, but it stopped her long enough for me to storm past her and plant myself between her and the door.

Her eyes were already wet with tears. *Shit.*

"I wasn't trying to push you off. I just don't want this"—I motioned to the mat—"to be the first time I'm with you." I took her hands in mine once more and gently coaxed them out of tight fists. "You have to believe that I'm done pushing you away. I don't have the strength to do it anymore. I've wanted you all this time, but I thought I wasn't good enough for you."

Lifting her hands up, once they finally opened, I kissed the palm of one hand, then the other, hating the little crescent-shaped marks I found there. "I still know I'm not good enough for you, but I realize now that no one is. But you need someone, and I want to be that someone."

I pulled her in my arms and lifted her up, kissing her softly on the lips before letting her back down on her feet. Her arms felt so good wrapped around my neck, her body still pressed against mine. The way it should be. We stood there for a moment, just looking into each other's eyes.

Her gaze left mine, and her forehead creased. "I have to tell Chris." She bit her lip.

Chris. He was going to fucking kill me. But when she looked up at me again with pouty eyes, I no longer gave a shit. Chris could beat me senseless if that was what it took for me to be with this angel. I leaned in to kiss her again, but my phone rang.

"Who keeps calling?" she asked.

"No one. It's just my sister, wanting to borrow money."

Twenty-Two

Ian had just completely rocked my world, shattering it into a million tiny pieces. His warm mouth on my core had been better than all the times I'd fantasized about him combined. And now he was looking at me with that hungry gaze of his and telling me that he wanted me. I could have melted right into the sea of blue mats in his gym.

Telling Chris about us wasn't going to be fun, but I'd wanted Ian for the better part of a year now and I felt like I had just won the damn lottery. He was so hot and sweet, and made me feel things I'd never felt before.

His phone started ringing yet again. He checked the phone before answering. "Sophia, what on earth is so important—" His brow wrinkled as he listened to her. I could hear the faint but frantic lilt of his sister's voice, but I couldn't tell what she was saying.

"Where are you?" he asked, his body tense as he listened. "Stay on the phone with me. I'm coming to get you. Just a second." He pulled the phone away from his face, his eyes filled with a mixture of panic and anger. "She was mugged. She says she's okay, but I need to go pick her up."

I nodded and grabbed my purse. "Let's go."

He shook his head. "No, I don't want you going. She's in a bad part of town."

"Your chivalry is endearing, but misguided. Remember where I live? Besides, she said she was okay, but would it hurt to have a nurse there?" I pointed at myself. "Just in case? She must be in shock, and might not realize she's injured."

His face grew even more fearful, and I wished I'd kept my mouth shut. I hadn't meant to suggest she was hurt.

"She's probably fine," I said, "but I can still help." I slipped my hand into his, and he squeezed it while he briefly mulled it over.

Finally, he nodded and led the way down to the parking garage while still holding the phone to his ear, talking to Sophia. The car alarm chirped as we approached his Escalade. I slid into the passenger side and he hopped into the driver's seat. Wasting no time, he brought the car to life.

Surprisingly he ended up driving to my neighborhood, taking the usual route he took when he drove me home, only about five times faster. As he took a residential corner at forty miles an hour, I tugged on the seatbelt to make sure it was tight.

His brow furrowed, his muscles tense, he somehow managed to sound levelheaded as he talked to Sophia on the drive over. About a mile from my place, he turned onto one of the worst streets in that part of town. I was used to my neighborhood, but if Sophia was a trust-fund kid like her brother, she was way out of her element.

We rounded the final corner and my heart almost broke. I had no idea what Sophia looked like, but I knew the girl on the bus bench was her. She wore expensive heels. Her dress was designer, and would have been gorgeous if it hadn't had black smudges on the bright yellow fabric, and a rip in the shoulder that would have exposed her if she hadn't been holding it up. Her eyes were smeared with runny makeup.

Ian was out of the car before I'd managed to free myself from the seatbelt. He was pumped. Angry. And a whole lot out of control. Even more so than when he was preparing for a fight, if that was possible.

"Ian, wait." I got out, following him to the bench where his sister sat. I hoped to God that whoever did that to her was already in police custody, because injury or not, Ian looked like he was going to kill someone. A vein throbbed in his neck, and his fists were clenched at his sides.

"Stay in the car, Kenzie," he growled.

I was tempted to obey since he was seriously pissed off, but I was more worried about his sister, so I followed at a safe distance.

"I told you, I don't remember what he looked like," Sophia was saying as I approached.

"Where were you when this happened?" Ian asked. He leaned over her with his hand on the back of the bench. His gaze darted around, looking for anyone who might seem the least bit suspicious. Now that he was near his sister, he seemed to relax the tiniest bit.

"I don't remember. I told you, I was dazed. I wandered a while before I thought to call you."

That was all I needed to hear. I scooted in on the bench next to her. "Sophia, my name is MacKenzie. I'm a nurse," I said. "Did you hit your head?"

"No." She turned away from me, but I caught a glimpse of her eyes and my heart almost broke for a second time. Her pupils were dilated and her eyes were red. That combined with the insane pace her knee was bouncing told me all I needed to know. She was using. Probably cocaine from the way she kept wiping at her nose.

I searched Ian's face for any indication that he knew his kid sister was coked-up out of her gourd, but it was clear he didn't. Not that I could blame him for missing it. After all, the signs of her recent assault were much more obvious.

"What happened?" I asked.

"I was attacked. I got away before anything happened, but I just want to go home."

"We should call the police," I said.

"No," they both said in unison, and Ian said, "I don't want this shit behind bars where I can't get to him."

Sophia whimpered. "Ian, it was nothing. I told you I don't remember who it was. Now can you please just drive me home?"

Ian surveyed the street one last time, then turned to his sister. "Yeah, let's get you home."

I tried to sit with Sophia in back, but she waved me off, saying she was fine, and pushed me to sit up front with Ian. She tried to get us to just drop her off, but Ian insisted on walking her upstairs and getting her settled.

"You don't mind, do you, Kenzie? I'm sorry to drag you all over town like this."

I shook my head. "No, not at all." I was worried for Sophia, and glad he wasn't just going to let her wander upstairs alone.

In the elevator, Sophia kept tapping her foot and bouncing against the wall, literally, by leaning back, then pushing off with her hands. It looked like she was going to explode any moment.

Ian and I followed her down the hall, and she opened the door. It was a nice enough apartment, well, probably a condo like Ian's, but there was clothing and dirty dishes strewn everywhere.

Ian scanned the place, and concern filled his eyes. "What happened here?"

"Nothing," she barked and tried to close the door on us, but Ian was having none of that. He pushed through the door, and I gave him some space before following.

He acted like this was all new, which meant he might not even know she was using. If she were my patient, I couldn't tell Ian, but neither she nor her insurance were paying for my services. I didn't want him to explode at her, though, so I watched him.

After wandering around to the various rooms, securing the apartment, Ian planted himself on the sofa. His eyes were sharp and he was about to snap, but not at her. He looked at her as if she was someone who needed protecting.

Ian could never hurt his sister. I would have to tell him; he could get her help.

"Just go, Ian," she said. "Thanks for coming to get me. I'm just gonna take a shower and crash for the night, nothing exciting going on here. Thank you and good-bye." She looked almost pissed.

I stepped forward. "Sophia, you and I both know he isn't going anywhere until you're cleaned up and he's calmed down. Let's go take a look at those scrapes."

I took her hand and guided her to the solitary hallway, which had to lead to the bathroom. When Ian got up to follow, I said, "I've got this, Ian. You just relax. This is a girl thing."

"Does Ian know?" I asked once the bathroom door had closed behind us.

Sophia folded her arms and turned away from me. "I don't know what you're talking about," was her snotty little response. She was trying to push me away by being cold. I'd seen it before; she was desperate to be left alone to feed her addiction.

Not on my watch.

"Oh, right," I said. I opened her medicine cabinet and started rummaging through the bottles of pills.

"Stop it." She reached for a bottle of antihistamine and I swatted her hand away, taking the same bottle off the shelf myself and opening it.

"Are your allergies acting up? You want some of this?" I asked, tipping the bottle's contents into my hand. No pills, just a small clear vial. It was almost empty, save for a tiny trace of powder. She reached for it, and I pulled it behind my back.

"Sophia, does Ian know you're using?"

She took a deep breath as if to fight off tears. "No, please don't tell him. He'll tell our parents. I hardly ever use, and…I can stop. I'll stop. I promise." Her eyes were wide, but not because she was scared. It was because of how high she was.

I lifted the toilet seat and opened the vial, tapping the last pinch of cocaine into the toilet. Her hands went for the vial as I did so.

This was bad, and so heart wrenching. I felt my fist balling up. I'd known so many addicts when I was a kid. Several of my foster parents were. I always tried to be nice and encouraging to them in the hopes that they would stop. It wasn't until nursing school that I learned addicts wouldn't get help until they were ready. Sometimes that meant tough love. So as much as I wanted to, I couldn't baby her.

"Clean yourself up," I said, then let myself out of the bathroom.

Her faint sobs followed me down the hall, begging me to turn back and tell her it would all be okay. God, I wanted to. But I went back to meet Ian in the living room. Addicts needed tough love.

When I got there, he was still seated on the sofa, his head in his hands. I wasn't sure what he was doing until I saw what was laid out in front of him on the coffee table. A CD case with a dusting of white powder.

I didn't have to tell him his little sister was snorting coke. The evidence was right in front of him.

Twenty-Three

IAN

How the hell did I not know?

The signs were all there. MacKenzie told me they weren't always easy to spot, but still, I should have seen them. Sophia was my little sister. I have known her all my life.

I thought back to the few times I'd seen Sophia in the past month. The way her leg had started bobbing up and down nervously, the irritability. She had been secretive, and had asked for more money. She was manipulative, even more so than usual. Only I hadn't noticed because I was so wrapped up in my own career, so focused on my stupid injury. So now, here I was on her sofa, waiting for her to come down from her high so we could talk.

MacKenzie had spent several hours going through Sophia's place. She picked up clothing, washed the dishes, did a load of laundry, and even mopped the floor. That, and everything else from the day had worn her out.

Now she lay next to me, her head in my lap, dozing quietly. I ran my fingers through her hair, so thankful she'd come with me. If she hadn't been here, I'd have lost my shit. MacKenzie took control of the situation in a way I never could have. I was so hell-bent on finding the guy who mugged Sophia so that I could exact revenge, I couldn't even see that there was something way more fucked-up going on. I don't know what I would have done if she hadn't been here.

Hell, I guess I do. I would have ignored the signs and run off half-cocked to find whoever did this to Sophia. I still wanted to figure out who the hell had put her on to that shit. And I would be finding out once she was clean; I had to wait until she came down. No matter how much I wanted to punch whoever did this shit to her, I had to fucking calm down.

I looked down again at Kenzie. She was curled up on her side in the fetal position next to me. I'd offered to get her a cab, but she refused, insistent that she would wait out Sophia's high with me.

I brushed my finger against her cheek. It was so soft. It brought me back to the moments we'd had together today before. I'd finally done it. I'd done what I had been wanting to do for the last six months, since the first night I met her—I committed myself to being everything I could be for her. God, it felt good to finally be able to give in to the need, to tell her how I felt about her.

MacKenzie stirred under my touch. "Sorry I dozed off. I meant to keep you company." She stretched and sat up, scooting in so she curled against my side.

"No, it's okay, you need rest." I looked into her sleepy eyes. "You have to work tomorrow."

That was the wrong thing to say. She groaned and buried her head in my shoulder.

My stomach sank. I wasn't the only one who was worried about how Chris would take this. I put my arms around her and kissed the top of her head, wishing there was some way we could avoid telling Chris, yet knowing I couldn't do that to him. He was a friend.

God, and this was all my stupid fault for pushing him at her. I practically served her to him. I was such a fucking douche-wad.

Twenty-Four

I'd never been sentimental about waking up next to a guy, and yet here I was curled up in Ian's arms, unwilling to open my eyes in case it might all be a dream.

I pressed my nose to his T-shirt, and the familiar scent of his detergent, body soap, and a hint of musk filled my senses. I traced my fingers over his chest and down his abs. Even as he slept, his breathing slow, I could still feel the definition in his muscles. My leg was draped over his groin, and he had the hint of morning wood.

My grip tightened around his chest, and I tried not to think about it. I still couldn't believe what had happened between us at his gym. The confident way he'd pulled my panties down my legs and licked my center... I shuddered and squeezed him tighter.

His sister lay sleeping in the next room; this wasn't the time. She'd finally dozed off at six in the morning, and we'd curled up to get in a few hours of sleep before we had to take Ian to the doctor.

My stomach growled. I was hungry, but I didn't want to move. Ian's breathing changed and his embrace tightened. I finally opened my eyes because I wanted to see his face.

It was perfect. His square jaw was covered in stubble, which was only a little shorter than his hair. His clear blue eyes looked down at me with so much tenderness.

"Hey, Kenzie." We closed the distance and kissed. "You ready to face the day?"

The reality of his words hit me. This was real. It wasn't a dream. He couldn't still want me this morning, could he? After all, this didn't happen to girls like me.

"Listen, what happened back at your place…we were caught up in the heat of the moment, I understand if you…" I was giving him a way out, shutting down these growing feelings I had for him before he had the chance to fracture my heart again.

His forefinger over my lips quieted me. "Don't pussy out on me now, Kenzie. I want this with you, I've wanted this for a long fucking time."

He kissed the top of my head. Something he'd only done a few times, but I loved it and hoped he would make a habit of it. God, he was so sweet.

"Oh my God. Will you guys get a fucking room?" Sophia stood over us, her hair all matted. She'd forgotten to remove her makeup, which was now smeared up and down her face.

"Morning, Sis." Ian sat up, and I followed. "You must have slept a whole five minutes." He slumped down and bent his head over, rubbing the back of his neck as if he'd just remembered he was supposed to be irritated with her. "This is it, Sophia. End of the road. If you can't stay clean, I'm kidnapping you and hauling your ass to rehab. Do I make myself clear?"

"Ian, you can't force me to go to rehab. Besides, I don't need it. I'm fine," she said.

"Do I make myself clear?"

She frowned and averted her eyes. "Yes."

"And that five grand I gave you really is the last you'll see from me. If you need more to get through the month, I'll buy you a case of ramen noodles. There won't be any more handouts."

"Ian, I was mugged yesterday. I really don't have any money left. The guy took it all."

His eyes got wide. "Sophia, what the hell were you doing walking around that part of town with five thousand dollars cash?" He chuckled to himself. "Never mind. I think I know." He started pulling his shoes on. "I have to go right now. I'll stop by later with your case of ramen."

"Ian," she whined.

He slid his hand into mine, ignoring his sister completely, and gave me a look that could melt butter. "You ready to go?"

I nodded. Even though I was in no way ready for the day—dealing with Chris and all—I understood what Ian was doing with Sophia. It was time for some tough love, and it was time to get on with the day. In fact, it was important to get on with this day, so that it would soon be over. Then I could spend the rest of my time with this seriously sexy man.

He stood up and helped me to my feet.

"Ian, wait," Sophia said.

He led me to the door, then turned back to her. "This is it, Sophia. You're cut off. You can't whine your way out of this one. I'll be by later to check on you. Be good. You can do this."

He gave his sister a hug and she squeezed him back, her eyes shut tight and her lower lip trembling. And with that we left.

Twenty-Five

MacKenzie

Ian pulled into the gym's parking lot and let the car idle. He'd hardly spoken since we'd left the doctor's office. I'd expected him to be silent. What I didn't expect was how unruffled and in control he was, considering what the doctor had just told him.

"This means no more self-defense classes until you're back on track," I said to break the silence.

He shook his head, but the corner of his mouth turned up, hinting at a smile. "If you think a bad report card from the doc will get you out of self-defense lessons, you are sorely mistaken." He slid his hand around mine and wove our fingers together. "I'll get myself back on track. Don't you worry about it. It's not your problem."

"But it is. Why do you think I'm coming to work with you twice a week?"

"Because you think I'll be good in bed," he said in a husky voice.

I blushed at how true his words were, but it made me laugh. "Maybe, but that's not the only reason." I traced my finger along his arm and looked at him. "This is something you've worked long and hard for. I want you to win. I want you to succeed."

He cupped my cheek with his hand, "I will win, MacKenzie. Anything you want."

I laughed. "You can't promise you'll win."

He shook his head. "I can. I'll do it for you. I'll win my fight. Promise." His eyes held mine, and I knew he would do anything to keep a promise to me. The thought warmed me.

Ian winning his fight wasn't the only thing I wanted. At that moment, I also wanted to straddle him and press my body against his, but I wasn't going to do that in front of Chris's gym. I still hadn't broken up with him. "Maybe I should start coming over every day to work with you."

"That sounds like a good idea." His voice was low, and I wondered if he was only holding back because of where we were. "Come over tonight and we'll…work on things."

I felt a throb between my legs. God, I wanted him to work on me.

But then my eye caught movement behind him and I sat up straight, pulling away from him. He turned to look. It was just a mom walking down the street with a double stroller, but it was enough to remind us of one of the issues we had to deal with today.

"Are you sure you don't want me to talk to Chris first?" he asked.

"No, it makes more sense if I let him down. If I don't and he finds out we're dating, it will be like we're cheating."

"We almost are."

"But it will only hurt him to put it that way. Maybe we should give him a while too before we tell him about us. Just to soften the blow a little. I'll talk to him today. And hopefully he'll be true to his word, and I'll still have a job."

"Chris is a good guy. He'd never fire you for breaking up with him."

Ian was probably right, but when Chris found out I was also dating his buddy Ian, I wasn't sure it would all remain cool between us. And I really wished I didn't have to test it out.

"Call me if things get intense and you need me to come get you." He squeezed my hand. "I'll come pick you up at the end of your shift so you don't have to bus over." He scanned the parking lot before leaning in, giving me a light kiss just below my jawline. I turned and took one last look at him before heading in.

In the fifteen seconds it took me to get to the front door, I'd determined that I was definitely going to talk to Chris first thing. Ripping off the Band-Aid seemed like the way to go. Besides, he deserved to know right away that it was over.

But by the time I'd made it through the gym to his office, I thought maybe it would be easier on him if I didn't tell him until the end of the day. Because then he wouldn't have to see me again until tomorrow. I was just spinning on my heel to get as far away from his office as I could when Chris called out to me.

"Hey, MacKenzie, did I see Ian drop you off just now?"

Every single muscle in me tensed. What had he seen? There was no way I would be able to act like nothing was going on. I was a lousy liar. If I was going to talk to him, I had to tell him.

I took a deep breath and turned back to the office. "Yeah, we just got back from his doctor visit."

I took a step just inside the office, scared that venturing farther would cause me to freak out. I had no clue why I was so worried about this. I had broken up with guys before. Granted, with most guys it was just after a few dates.

Chris and I had been seeing each other for a month, which wasn't long for most people, but it was nearing a record for me. And then there was that whole boss thing. I'd never dated a boss, and thus never had to break up with one before. Maybe that was why my stomach was wound up so tightly that puking didn't seem out of the question.

"Well, come on in and tell me how it went," he said, smiling and at ease.

He had no idea. Must not have seen anything. Thank goodness.

I shuffled in a few more feet, taking a seat on the edge of the couch.

"So, how's our man doing?" He leaned forward, folding his arms on the desk. His giant body dwarfed the desk, making it look dainty.

"It could have gone better," I said. "The doctor wants Ian to wait another week before he begins sparring again." This was a serious blow. The fight was only three weeks away, and he needed to be working on his strength and sharpening his skills, but the doctor didn't think he was ready.

Chris ran his hand over his clean-shaven head, and his forehead creased. "That's not good." He winced. "I was worried about this happening."

I looked down at the floor. "I feel like I could have done a better job working with him."

"Don't worry, MacKenzie, this isn't on you. I was just hoping it wouldn't come to this." He picked up a pencil and started tapping it on the desk.

"Come to what?" I asked.

"I think I'm going to have to replace Ian in the fight."

"What? No. He's worked so hard for this."

"Yeah, but we knew this was a possibility. Why do you think I brought in Jonah?"

"You said you brought him in to work with Ian."

He shrugged. "Yeah, but I kept him here because I knew we might need him to fight in Vegas. And it looks like I was right."

Damn it. That wasn't the reason he told me before. Why was he giving up on Ian so quickly? I thought they were friends.

"I don't think it's as bad as I made it sound, Chris," I said. "We've still got time to get him in shape. I was going to start working with him every day to make sure he stays on track." I realized I was wringing my hands and I stopped, placing them on my knees.

"You really are invested in this, aren't you?"

I shrugged, then nodded. "I think he can get there. He wants to, and he will. I would like to help. It's my job, right?"

It was so much more than that to me. I wanted to see hard work and determination pay off. It was like that alone could restore my faith in humanity. Ian should be at this fight. He should win this fight.

Chris smiled warmly and leaned forward, tilting his head to the side. "My little Kenzie has herself a project," he said. "I guess I wouldn't be a very good boyfriend if I didn't at least give you a chance to see your mission through." He got up and moved around the desk, taking a seat next to me. "If you think he's got it in him, you've got the next week to prove it. If the doctor doesn't clear him for sparring by then, I'm sorry, sweetie, but I'll have to put Jonah in."

He slid his arm around my waist and pulled me in. I didn't resist, going limp in his arms. I stared at the floor, digesting what he'd just said.

All the thoughts I had about breaking up with Chris moved to the back of my mind. He was right on the edge of removing Ian from the fight. I wouldn't give him any more reason to do so.

He pulled away to look at me. "You look tired. Did you sleep okay last night?"

I shook my head. "I had a hard time getting to sleep." It was the truth, but my omission of all the details of the evening with Ian and his sister seemed like maybe the worst lie I'd ever told.

"Why don't you take the day off? You should go home and get some rest."

I nodded.

"We're still on for Friday, right?"

"Yeah," I said. We exchanged a quick kiss, and I pulled myself up off the couch and headed home.

Twenty-Six

IAN

I'd planned on picking MacKenzie up at three, so I was surprised when she showed up at my building just after lunch. Her eyes were puffy, as if she'd been sleeping.

"Did you come from the gym?" I asked when I let her into my workout room.

She shook her head. "No, Chris let me go home to get some sleep."

It felt like there was something she wasn't telling me, but she didn't seem upset, maybe just dazed from a long nap. "He didn't fire you, did he?"

"No." She shook her head again, then took a seat on one of the workout benches. She took a deep breath before she continued. "I didn't break up with him."

Something about the way she was looking at me made my stomach fall. "Why not?" I knew as I asked the question that I didn't want to hear the answer.

"Because it didn't feel right."

I ran my hand over my hair and waited for her to say more.

"I'm sorry. I think I'm going to stay with Chris." Her voice was softer now, and she looked down at the floor. She was sitting on her hands, so I couldn't read the telltale sign if she was upset, but she was definitely uncomfortable.

She'd chosen Chris.

I forced out a breath, looking down at the floor as well. I swallowed hard against a tightness in my throat, my jaw clenched. Rage boiled inside me, just under the surface, but I couldn't lose it. Not right here, not right now. This was her choice. I was the douche-roll who passed on her when I had the chance. I had no right to give her shit about what she wanted.

"Okay."

She looked up at me, as if she was surprised at my reaction. "Okay?"

I nodded. "Okay. Chris is still my friend, and I hope you are too. I want you to be happy. If he makes you happy," I said and forced myself to shrug. "Then sure…it's okay."

She let out a breath she'd been holding. "Good. I was hoping you wouldn't be too upset, because here's the thing—I still want to help you work on your shoulder. Every day, like we talked about."

Surprised, I ran my hand along the back of my neck, kneading my shoulder. She had to be kidding if she thought I would be willing to work with her after all we'd been through. After how much she knew I wanted her.

I started to shake my head, but then inexplicably switched to nodding. "Okay," I said again, at a loss for anything more.

I must be a fucking tool, but I realized that if I couldn't be with her, if she couldn't be mine, I could at least spend time with her in this way. And that was better than nothing.

Damn, I fucking loved to punish myself.

MacKenzie

I'd barely held it together as I worked for several hours with Ian on his strength exercises, but at least we had something else to focus on.

When it came time for him to drive me home, I had to sit on my hands. Ian had figured out why I balled up my hands in fists; somehow he knew that meant I was upset. So I determined that anytime I was about to cry, I would sit on my hands. That way he couldn't see it, couldn't see how I felt, because he couldn't know my true motivations for staying with Chris. If he did, my plan wouldn't work. I needed him to think I was done with him so he would forget about me and focus on the fight.

Forget about me. The thought was sobering, but given my past, was something I was accustomed to. Chris had made it clear that the only reason he was still considering letting Ian fight was because he wanted to humor me as his "girlfriend." So if I wanted Ian to fight, I'd have to remain Chris's girlfriend whether I wanted to be or not, and I definitely did *not*. But what choice did I have?

I felt so empty that I had to lock my arms straight in order to hold myself up as he drove. We talked about strategy in the car, and then on the way up the steps to my apartment.

"So I'll come by your place after work tomorrow," I said.

Ian shook his head. "I've been thinking it might be time for me to move back to Chris's gym. After all, I have most of my strength back. I'd like to at least be around the other fighters, even if I can't fight too."

"Sure." I nodded. That made sense. And maybe it would help if I didn't have to be alone with him. I would have to be better about hiding the longing in my eyes and focus on my job. "Well then, I'll see you tomorrow at the gym."

I pulled my key out of my purse and unlocked my door, opening it. Then I turned back to look at Ian. He was quiet for a moment, and I caught myself remembering the first night he'd walked me to my door. How protective he was when he thought I was in danger. How he'd stepped in front of me.

My heart thumped unevenly. Resisting the urge to sink into his broad chest and wrap my arms around his waist, I turned away and faced my door.

"Good night," he said.

I walked inside and locked the door behind me, knowing he wouldn't leave until he heard that click. Dropping my keys and purse on the floor, I dragged myself into the living room and sank down onto the sofa, curling up into a ball. I held in the first sobs, not wanting him to hear, but as his footsteps faded down the hallway, the tears began to flow, and I couldn't help the cries escaping. I hugged a pillow close to my chest and let go, my body releasing sob after sob. My head hurt and my chest ached—actually ached. This was why I never let anyone get close to me. Because it effing hurt.

I'd realized how easily Ian could lose Chris's sponsorship in the Vegas fight. Ian had been training for this his whole life, and Chris wanted to take him out of the fight even before he knew we were together. There was no way he'd continue to back Ian if he found out I was leaving him for Ian, which was why he could never know. And why breaking things off with Ian was the only thing to do.

So when Chris sent me home to sleep, I spent the morning crying my heart out. I cried until I was numb, and then I cried some more, because I had to get it out of my system if Ian was going to believe that I wanted to stay with Chris. And before I left, I'd loaded on the eye makeup and the eye drops, and given myself a pep talk. I was good at pretending like things were normal when they weren't. I could do this.

And I did, but I barely made it through. Breaking up with Ian had been the hardest thing I'd ever done. Working next to Ian after that, without being able to be with him, was even harder. But I'd made it through. And tomorrow I would too. Maybe each day, if I was lucky, it would get a little easier, because I couldn't imagine how anything could feel any worse.

Now that I knew the sweet side to Ian, his protective streak, and that he felt the same way about me as I did about him, it made this a hundred times harder. And of course I tortured myself the entire time we worked together as little memories seeped into my brain—his full lips nipping at mine, the large bulge below his navel pressing insistently into me...

But Ian was no longer just the addictively hot MMA fighter I wanted to bang the living daylights out of. He was more. Much more.

Twenty-Seven

IAN

I was worried about moving back to the gym, worried I'd be tempted to push myself too hard, or jump right into sparring. And as valid as those reasons were, the biggest problem was that I didn't think I could handle another round of one-on-one with MacKenzie unless I had the safety of other people around. It wasn't that I couldn't respect her choice, I would never force myself on her or anyone, but the simple thought of being alone with her and not able to touch her depressed the fuck out of me.

The next morning I headed to the gym early. I wasn't supposed to work with Kenzie until later in the afternoon, but I planned on getting in a good workout. I might not be able to use my left arm yet to its full potential, but I could abuse the shit out of my other three limbs, and every other muscle in my body. Something I'd been doing at my home gym every day, five or six hours a day, but looked forward to doing back at the full gym. I could hammer on a punching bag in my gym until my arms fell off, but something about being back with the guys pushed me even harder.

As I walked in, I instantly regretted telling Chris I was planning on coming back today. I was greeted by a banner that read, WELCOME BACK, PUSSY! I should have known. The dipshit had the banner made a while back, and he pulled it out anytime one of the guys came back from an injury or a long absence. I guess it was my turn to experience the humiliation.

MacKenzie was usually there first thing in the morning, so I was surprised to not see her when I arrived. I told myself it was a good thing she wasn't there, because then I could focus on my training, but part of me couldn't get past worrying about where she was.

The new guy, Jonah, was lifting when I got there. He saw me, put the weights down, and came over. "Hey, Ian."

"Hey," I said. We'd met briefly when I was in the gym a week ago to talk to Chris. A few pro fighters were douche-rods outside of the ring; thankfully, he was not one of those.

"A little bird told me you might be coming back to the gym this morning." He smiled and looked up at the banner on the far end of the gym.

"Really." I laughed.

"Anyway, the same little bird suggested you might be looking for some help with your submission and grappling technique. If you want to, we can work on that."

That was actually a great idea. I needed to get back into strategies and fighting as soon as possible. I couldn't start sparring yet, but that didn't mean I couldn't work on technique.

I gladly followed him over to a mat to work on submissions, which was my weakest skill, and something I had to work on even harder now that I was coming out of an injury. Everyone knew the best way to get a fighter to tap out if he'd been recently injured was to go after that injury. And that meant I had to be ready for my opponent to try to fuck with my shoulder. First order of business was definitely working on getting out of and staying out of submission holds.

We set up on a mat on the far side of the gym near the locker room.

"Okay," Jonah began, "let's start by showing you some holds I use and the best way to get out of them. Go ahead and lie down."

I lay on the mat, and he knelt over me and went through the motions of pulling my arm into the first hold. I caught myself looking across the room at the empty treadmill and wondering where MacKenzie was. I hoped she was okay.

Damn. I needed to get my mind off her and focus on the fight.

Jonah moved quickly, slipping his legs around me and pulling my good arm in a direction it was not supposed to go. "Okay, how do you get out of this?" he asked.

I looked around for some part of him to punch, but he was behind me and all his good targets were protected. And I couldn't twist out of his hold because of the angle at which he held my arm. Fuck, this was why I never let them get me on the ground in the first place. This was also why I needed to train with Jonah.

I pushed up with my legs and tried to roll on top of him, but he held me down so that I might as well be fighting a brick wall.

"Use your other arm," he said. "I've got your arm in a vice, but if you distract me by pushing up, I won't be able to control what your other arm does. Use that."

I pushed up against him again and realized right away what he was getting at. In order to keep me down, he was pushing forward, which made his head very vulnerable. I reached up and hooked him into a chokehold, pulling him around in front of me.

He tapped out. "Good. Let's try that again."

When we moved back into position, I noticed Chris stepping out of his office, followed by

MacKenzie. He said something and she laughed, but it seemed forced. She still looked tired, but maybe a little bit more relaxed than she was the day before.

As I lay there on the mat, I studied them as a couple. Something pricked at the back of my mind as I noted the distance between them, the way all their interactions seemed forced. She was never like that with me. You could light a city block with the electricity that buzzed between us.

But it didn't matter. She'd chosen him.

Chris noticed me and waved me over.

"I guess we'll have to finish working on this later," I said to Jonah. "Thanks for the help. I'll really need it if I'm going to win in Vegas."

"Yeah. I don't know if Chris told you, but I might be going with you. He wants me to be your cornerman."

"That would be great. I could use an expert on submissions on my side."

"That road goes both ways. I hear you're a mean pounder, and I'd love to get some pointers on boxing."

"Sure." I headed off toward the office.

"Welcome back, pussy," Chris said when I was within shouting distance. He looked up at the party banner hung up at the front of the gym and smiled. The little shit.

I laughed. "It's good to be back." We bumped fists and he led the way back into his office, taking a seat behind his desk.

Chris grinned at me. "I was going to get you a cake, but your ass is in training mode."

I wasn't sure if it was the tone of his voice or what, but at that moment I was reminded of the fact that I'd gotten his girlfriend off the other day. My mouth and fingers had been inside his girl, and we'd been moments away from having sex.

I was pretty sure MacKenzie hadn't told him about that. But it suddenly occurred to me that I should know for sure before allowing myself to be alone with this guy. He might not fight pro anymore, but he was a weight class above me, and could probably whip my ass with my arm out of commission.

But Chris didn't hint at knowing anything about what happened between Kenzie and me, he just tossed me one of his famously nasty homemade protein shakes and leaned back in his chair.

Ugh, I didn't miss these. Still, I shook it up and chugged it, trying to assess the situation.

"MacKenzie told me how the doctor visit went, and I wanted you to know that I'm behind you in this. I've asked all the guys at the gym to help out. We're going to get you in shape for the next doctor visit."

Chris was a good friend. Knowing that he'd had my back this whole time made me feel even shittier about trying to take MacKenzie away from him. He was, after all, a decent guy, and she deserved that.

"Thanks," I said. "I'm excited to get back into it. I know I can be ready."

"Good. That's just what I wanted to hear. I saw you were out there training with Jonah, and I don't want to keep you from it, but I just talked to MacKenzie and I had to share. I don't know if you knew this or not, but things are going kinda slow with MacKenzie and me. For a while there, I thought maybe she wasn't into me, or there was someone else."

I shrugged, trying to keep my shit together. I didn't have a clue in hell where he was going with this, and was thankful that he'd remained seated. Maybe it wouldn't be a bad idea to talk to MacKenzie about what Chris knew. For the safety of everyone.

"Well, that's about to change." He got a smug grin on his face as he nodded like I knew what he was talking about. "She just agreed to go to Vegas with me."

I forced a smile and gritted out, "Great."

I wanted to come clean with Chris. As a friend, I knew I should, but I was starting to wonder if his knowing would do more harm—to him and the rest of us—than good. Besides, they were finally taking their relationship to the next level. Maybe it was best to just leave it alone.

As all these thoughts swirled around inside my head, I realized I was irritated that I couldn't be happy for him, and for them. And I desperately wanted to be.

I also wanted to fucking punch something. Repeatedly.

Twenty-Eight

IAN

Winning the fight in Vegas was crucial, but that didn't mean I was going to forget about Sophia. Family was important. I'd lost sight of that for a while, and ended up missing how messed up Sophia's life had become. I vowed that would never happen again. Not on my watch. Because if it was a choice between the fight in Vegas and saving my kid sister from doing drugs, Sophia would win, hands down.

But I didn't plan on it getting to that point.

Ever since I'd found out Sophia was snorting that shit, I'd been checking in with her face-to-face every evening. She seemed clean, as was evidenced by how exhausted and bitchy she was. She continued to nag me about lending her money, but that was not going to happen. Instead, I took her grocery shopping and paid her bills. She also wouldn't stop whining about how bored she was, so in order to shut her up, I took her along with me to go drinking with Cade.

Cade was already there, seated at one of the cracked red leather booths when we arrived. "You look like shit," he said as Sophia and I slid in across from him. The comment could have been targeted at Sophia since she did look like hell, but he knew better than to insult my kid sister. The douche was talking to me.

I rubbed my hand over my hair. "Fuck, man. At least let me get a beer in me before you start talking trash." I signaled for the waitress and ordered. "A light tap for me and a cola for her."

Sophia pouted, but she was only nineteen. I was no idiot, I knew she had a fake ID and drank all the time, but she wouldn't be doing it on my watch.

"Sophia, I'm surprised to see you hanging out with losers like us. What gives?" Cade winked at her as if it was an innocent question rather than an acknowledgment of the elephant in the room.

"Ian thinks I have some sort of 'problem' just because I like to have a good time." She glared at me, but it didn't matter what kind of mood she was in, she couldn't pass up a chance to see Cade. She'd always harbored a schoolgirl crush on him. "He's trying to make up for our parents being gone all the time." She shrugged and a hint of a smile came to her face. "You know Ian. His intentions are great enough to save the world, but he's too stupid to focus his energy in the right direction."

"Speaking of misguided idiots, what's going on with you and MacKenzie?" Cade asked.

I took a long pull on my beer before I could answer. "I don't know which one of us you're calling an idiot, but MacKenzie is off-limits as a topic of conversation. You want to talk about your girlfriend's menstrual cycle or your new fuckin' skin moisturizer, whatever, just not MacKenzie." It was going to be hard enough to see her with Chris at the gym every day. I was done talking about my feelings on the issue.

Cade was stunned somewhat silent. I took the opportunity to pound the rest of my beer and waved the waitress over. "Another one of these." It was one of the last nights I could drink before full training mode kicked in, and I planned to spend it somewhat inebriated. Maybe even make Sophia drive me home.

Sophia took a sip of her soda, then looked up at me. "Is that the chick you were making out with on my sofa?"

Fuck. "Sophia, damn it, we're not talking about this."

Cade leaned forward over the table. "Who were you making out with on her couch?"

I shook my head and blew out a breath, noting the waitress was headed back to our table with my fresh beer. *Thank God.*

"Ian?" Cade said.

I accepted my beer from the waitress. "Thanks. Keep 'em coming." I chugged another half beer and put the glass down on the table a little too hard, making Cade jump. "If I give you the basics of the Kenzie situation, you have to shut the fuck up about it when I'm done so that we can move on to more pleasant conversations such as how to rip the limbs off my next opponent."

Cade nodded, looking pleased with himself. "Done."

"I didn't mean to take your advice, but it happened. I just couldn't push her away anymore, and we fell into each other's arms during one of the self-defense lessons."

Sophia giggled. "You were giving a girl one-on-one self-defense lessons and didn't think it would lead anywhere?" She turned to Cade. "My brother's an idiot."

I kicked her under the table.

"Ouch," she cried, even though it was only a tap.

"She's dating Chris. I was giving her lessons because she lives in a bad part of town. The only reason I let it go as far as it did was because I thought she wasn't really into Chris. I thought she would leave him. But she didn't, she stayed with him. So now I feel like the biggest prick in the world. Having pushed myself on her when she didn't want to be with me, and trying to move in on Chris's girlfriend."

I finished my beer, hoping that the waitress would hurry with my next one. I couldn't be drunk enough to have this stupid fucking conversation.

"Huh," Cade said. He looked at his beer as if he was digesting what I'd just said. But then his brow wrinkled. "Promise you won't punch me?"

"No, I'm not promising anything. Out with it."

"Alexa was sure the two of you were together. She told me yesterday that she's been waiting for you two to get on with it for over a month. Said MacKenzie was driving her nuts, and she was so stoked that you had finally gotten there."

"Dude." My stomach was tightening, and it wasn't just because Cade was wearing on my last nerve. "It doesn't matter what Alexa thought. The only thing that matters is that MacKenzie made her choice."

Sophia snorted. "No way that chick likes someone else. She was giving you the sickest love-me eyes I've ever seen, and the way her body moved with yours? It was like a dance." She leaned toward Cade. "And the look on his face was something." She nodded her head toward me. "I've never seen him like that with any woman before. He was so pussy-whipped, I almost wanted to slap him out of it. That was some disgusting shit to witness."

"Sophia—" I started, but stopped short.

I wanted to call her out on the fact that she'd been high, and there was no way she could trust whatever it was what she thought she saw. But that was a shitty thing to say, and I was trying to be nice to Sophia, no matter how bitchy she was. I wasn't going to take her bait. Besides, if I had to be honest, she'd been right on at least one count. For the sixteen hours that MacKenzie and I had been together, for the time I thought she was mine, I'd been totally whipped.

But I had to respect MacKenzie's choice. "She wants to be with Chris, she said so to my face. It's time for me to realize I missed my chance and move on."

At that moment, I realized I wasn't just telling Sophia and Cade, I was telling myself. It really was time for me to get over it and move on.

Fuck.

Twenty-Nine

There was one important thing I learned as a kid going through foster care. Anytime I made friends at school, I'd have to leave them. Anytime I bonded with the other kids in one of the homes, something would happen and we'd all have to be moved, be separated. The lesson I learned was that if you got too emotionally attached to something, you would lose it. So as a rule I kept my emotions at a distance.

Until Ian. This whole time, I knew he was a threat to my carefully crafted way of life. Because being around him felt so good, I knew I was in danger of losing him. For some stupid reason, I thought I could keep the emotional demons at bay, but I'd gotten too comfortable with him, and he'd snuck past my defenses somehow. Sneaky bastard.

Rather than succumb to the pain of losing Ian, I switched to my other fantastic defense mechanism. I shut down my emotions and allowed myself to become comfortably numb. It had been a while since I'd had to shut off my emotions entirely, but I didn't see any other way of keeping Ian—and my feelings for him—in check.

I clenched my jaw, marched over to the weights, and pointed at the forty-five pounder. It was day two of us working together at the gym.

"It's time to start upping your game," I said.

I'd been going easy on Ian. Too easy. I was afraid he'd get hurt if I pushed him too hard during our previous sessions. It was because of that, because of my poor judgment, that he was in this mess now. I was going to make sure he got through it. I would make it right, even if that meant being hard on him. Whatever it took.

Just last week I wouldn't have had the strength to push him, but now that I had switched off my emotions, being a hard-ass was easy.

He looked at me as if he wanted to protest.

I rolled my eyes and grabbed the weight with both hands, heaving it off the weight stand.

Ian rushed over to me. "Don't do that. Let me get it." He tried to take it from me with his good arm, and I turned away.

"If you want this, take it, but only with your left hand." I turned to face him again. The weight was dang heavy; even with two hands, I was barely able to hold it up. It forced me into a hunched bent-knee position, but I held strong.

His jaw clenched and his eyes darkened. He was getting upset. Good. Maybe if he was angry, he would be able to push himself harder. "Just let me—"

"Uh-uh." I took a seriously labored step back. "The left hand. Your ligaments have healed. The only reason you can't fight yet is because your strength isn't where the doctor wanted it to be. So, please take this thing before I drop it on my foot."

He lunged in and grabbed it easily with his right hand. "Don't be stupid, MacKenzie," he barked.

"Stop being a baby," I barked back. "We don't have time for your pussyfooting around anymore, Ian."

I was shouting. *Crap*. I wanted him to work harder, but not if I had to turn into Bitchzilla to make it happen. I turned away and took a deep breath, trying to calm myself. Damn it, couldn't he see I just wanted him to win? Why did I always have to end up being such a dysfunctional mess?

His rough hand closed on my shoulder, and he gently kneaded it. "MacKenzie, I'm sorry."

For a moment I closed my eyes and allowed myself to imagine what it would be like to turn and face him, to have him sweep me into his arms and hold me to him. How good it would feel to press against his firm body and look longingly into his eyes.

I allowed myself only a moment of weakness to imagine this, then took another step away from him, shrugging off his hand before turning back to face him.

His hand fell to his side. "I didn't mean you were stupid. I know I need to work harder. Look." He pointed to his left hand, where he held the weight. "I want to do this. I need your help to get my strength back so that I can win this fight."

"Good," I said. "Let's see you do four sets of twelve." I waited for him to protest the extra set of reps I added on, but he didn't. Instead, he started in on his first rep.

Ian went through the first set without too much effort. With one arm, he shrugged up the weight I'd almost dropped as if it were as light as a can of soup. It was the third and fourth sets that almost killed him. He grunted through the final shrugs, something I should have been pushing him to do several weeks ago.

As he pushed through the final one, I caught sight of Chris just behind him coming out of the office with a woman I'd never seen before. She was about my age, maybe a little younger. Her hair was bleached blond, and she had serious makeup issues. Like her face was all deep tan, and her neck was seriously pink and pale.

Earth to Blondie, you can *put makeup on your neck. Or just less makeup on your face.* I wasn't the beauty police, but seeing someone trying and failing so hard kind of made me smirk.

The smirk fell when I saw what she was doing with her hand. She was resting it on Chris's abdomen, and Chris wasn't stopping her. In fact, he seemed as if he was used to having it there. She giggled and smiled at something he said, and he looked at her with something like satisfaction.

My mind raced, wondering if I'd seen them go into the office. Ian and I had been just outside for a good half hour, and I hadn't seen them go in. How long had they been in there?

Chris looked up and saw me staring. His posture immediately stiffened and he stepped out of Blondie's reach, putting on a smile for me. He said a few words to Blondie. She glared at me for a beat before she ran off, and Chris headed toward us.

"Hey, guys. How's the training going?" Chris said.

Ian turned to meet him. "Good. Your girlfriend is kicking my ass into shape."

Chris nodded and stepped forward, taking my hand. "Good. I knew there was something special about her when Cade introduced us."

I let him take my hand and forced a smile. And when he leaned in for a kiss, I kissed him back.

It was obvious something was off with the way he acted around Blondie, but when I searched my feelings, I found I didn't care. In fact, it was almost a relief. Because if Chris was cheating on me, it meant I had nothing to worry about.

The whole time I'd told myself I would be able to trick Ian into thinking I was happy with Chris, I was seriously conflicted about one thing—I'd thought Chris was a good guy, and I wasn't sure if I could continue to pretend with him. It felt like betrayal.

But now I knew. He was a douche-bag, just as horrible as I was. Maybe we deserved each other.

When he bent down to kiss me, I allowed it despite feeling not at all into it. Maybe this was what I deserved.

Thirty

MACKENZIE

It was Thursday, our usual girls' night. I'd begged off, telling Alexa I wasn't in the mood, and was just curling up on my sofa with a blanket and a pint of ice cream when my buzzer rang. I considered ignoring it, but it could be one of my neighbors. A woman down on the second floor was always locking herself out.

I peeked out the window at the stoop to find Ty and Alexa staring up at me. *Shoot*. Couldn't a girl have a night alone without her friends freaking out?

I buzzed them up and unlocked my door, plopping back down on the couch to wait for them.

Ty's giggling preceded them as they came to my door and then knocked.

"It's open."

"Hey, sweetie," Alexa said as she came in, brandishing two unopened bottles of my favorite cheap chardonnay, one in each hand. "Where's your corkscrew?"

Ty followed her in. "I brought shots." He laughed and held up a big mixing bowl with a cover on it.

"What kind of shots come in a mixing bowl?" I asked.

"I tried to make Jell-O shots. But I didn't have time to let the Jell-O set, so it's more like vodka infused with strawberry-flavored sugar." He followed Alexa into the kitchen, where both of them made themselves at home. "They're really good. I've had like two of them already."

"Three if you count the one you had while mixing the stuff," Alexa shouted loud enough for me to hear. I heard the clanking of metal as someone dug through my utensil drawer.

"Where's your corkscrew, lady?" Alexa asked again.

I sighed, replaced the lid on my pint of ice cream, and headed into the kitchen.

"You're looking too hard, Alexa," I said when I saw her digging around like a fool in my utensil drawer. Meanwhile, my corkscrew was out on the counter in front of her.

"Oh, there you are," she said to the corkscrew, plucking it off the counter like it was her new best friend.

"Which one of you drove?" I asked.

"I did." Alexa turned toward me as she worked the corkscrew into the cork. "I haven't had anything to drink—yet."

"And why are you guys here?"

"We were worried," she said. "You tried to duck out on girls' night."

"So?"

"You live for girls' night," Ty said. "I knew there was something wrong the second Alexa told me you weren't coming. So I said, 'We should go check on her. She would do the same thing for us.' So here we are."

"So here we are," Alexa echoed as she poured a glass of wine for me and another for herself. "So, what's up?"

Oh crap. They were going all intervention on me again. *Please, no.*

"Can't I just have a night at home alone? Does there need to be something wrong with me?"

"No," Ty said. "But there *is* something wrong, I can tell by your lousy makeup job. You've got ten times your usual cover-up around the eyes, and I can still see they're all puffy from crying."

I frowned. I'd been tear-free for most of the evening, save for the tiny crying jag right after I got home. But I was getting better. In fact, just before they showed up, I'd decided that tonight was my last night of grieving. Tomorrow I would pull myself up by my bootstraps and suck it up. Tonight was my last night of self-pity. And apparently they weren't going to let me go through it alone.

"I was having some PMS issues," I said pointedly, hoping that the mention of girly moodiness would make him back off.

"You don't get PMS," Alexa said, "you said so yourself. If you don't want to talk about it right now, that's fine, but you're drinking with us whether you want to or not." She handed me a glass of wine and a lowball full of red liquid. "Drink," she ordered.

I rolled my eyes at her and threw back the shot, almost choking on how sweet it was. "Geez, Ty, did you add enough sugar to this?" I chased the shot with some wine.

Alexa placed another shot in front of me, holding one for herself too. "We have to catch up to Ty."

She held up her glass and I toasted her, throwing back another ridiculously sweet shot. My tolerance was better than either of theirs, and getting Alexa drunk was always fun to watch, so I decided to play along. She wiped her mouth on her sleeve and went back to the mixing bowl to get us each another shot, ladling the jellied liquid out with a spoon.

Two hours and countless sugar/vodka shots later, we were all on my living room floor with a seriously juvenile case of the giggles. None of us could even remember what we were laughing about, but I was suddenly struck with how awesome they both were to have cared enough to come over and get me wasted in my time of need.

"I really love you guys. You know that, right?"

"Aw," Alexa sang. "We love you too, sweetie."

"I mean it. I needed this. Things were just getting too messed up at the gym, you know? Ever since the day I screwed up and let things get out of hand with Ian, he's been all awkward with me, and now I'm hiding things from Chris."

"Hang on." Ty held up his hand to stop me. "You're dating Ian, right?"

I shook my head. "I'm dating Chris. I just screwed up with Ian."

Alexa's eyes widened and she turned to me. "But if you never broke up with Chris, who was the blond girl Cade and I saw him with the other night? They were all over each other. Seriously, they needed to get a room."

I thought back to the girl I'd seen come out of the office with Chris. It had to be Blondie, but if Alexa had confirmation that Chris was cheating on me, that could get back to Ian. And I needed everything to maintain status quo until his fight was over.

I shrugged. "I don't know, maybe it wasn't Chris. Or the girl was his sister?"

Alexa frowned for a moment, looking like she was considering it. Maybe she was just drunk enough to go for it.

I looked down at my hands. Now I was lying to Alexa and Ty. First Chris, then Ian, and now my best friends. When had life become so complicated? How had things gotten this messed up?

One thing was for sure—I couldn't maintain this much longer. As soon as Ian's fight was over, I needed to end it with Chris, and maybe even find a new job.

Thirty-One

I was glad to be back at the gym. Not only was it good for me to be around other people again—a great distraction from MacKenzie—but I'd also been pushing myself harder.

Part of that was thanks to MacKenzie. She'd been killing me, adding extra sets and upping the weights every day. At first I thought she was doing it to push me away, but after a few days of her coming back again and again, I realized it wasn't that at all; she was giving me the push I needed to pass my next physical. I was thankful to her for that.

Still, by the end of the fourth day back at the gym, my body was so brutalized that when I got home around seven, I hardly had enough energy to feed myself before stumbling into bed. Not that I could go out partying anyway; I was back in full training mode. But I was so shit tired I fell asleep before my head hit the pillow.

I woke to the sound of my phone in the dead of night. I used to turn off the ringer before bed, but because of recent events, I'd cranked up the volume so that if my sister called, I would hear it.

My arm muscles screamed from the day's workout as I fumbled for my phone on the nightstand. The clock said it was only ten thirty, but my body and mind were of the opinion that it must be much later.

"Yeah," I grumbled when I finally found the answer button.

"Is this Ian?" a man's voice asked.

I pulled the phone away to see who was calling. My phone said it was Sophia. I shot up in bed. "Who is this?"

"Ian…" There was a pause. "Don't get too excited. It's Rick."

"Rick?" My brain was too fucking tired to figure out what was going on. "Rick who? Where's Sophia?"

"Rick, Cade's buddy from the adult-film industry. Sophia's here with me. She's safe, but you need to come get her."

I was so upset I couldn't fucking speak. All I wanted to do was reach through the phone and strangle Rick. I actually held the phone away from my ear for a second, trying to figure out if there was some way to achieve that magical feat. But there wasn't.

"Just tell me where you are and I promise not to kill you." *Just torture you to within an inch of your life, that's all.*

"Hey, I called *you*, remember? I haven't touched her. I don't know how she found my studio, but she showed up with some guy asking if she could work for me."

"Don't you dare hire her. I will end you," I yelled.

"Are you kidding me? I remember our last meeting, the one where you dragged me out of Sara's apartment by the arm and told me not to touch your little sister. I value my life, which is why I contacted you as soon as I could."

"How did you get her phone?" I asked.

"I lifted it from her purse. Listen, in order to keep her here, I had to tell her I'd hire her, so you need to get your ass over here soon and pull her out. Right now I have one of the techs giving her a tour of our facilities, but I won't be able to stall her here much longer."

"Just tell me where and I'll be there," I said and got up, pulling on clothes as I talked.

He gave me the address, and I was about to hang up so that I could plug the location into my phone.

"One more thing," he said. "I think she might be coked up."

"How the hell did she get that? I better not find out she got it from you."

"No. Like I said, I value my life. But the guy she came here with seems a little shady. I told my guys to get rid of him."

"Don't," I said.

"No. We're not keeping him here for you, sorry. I run a clean operation here, and can't have you murdering some loser on my property. He'll be gone by the time you get here. I have a business to run."

I sighed. "Fine, but if by some miracle he's still there when I get there, you will have a mess to clean up."

I hung up, pulled up my GPS, and plugged in the address as I made my way down to the garage and hopped into my car.

Red.

All I could see was the color red. Luckily, my body seemed to be able to operate the vehicle, even though I'd fucking lost it. The address was a good twenty miles away, but I made it there in ten minutes.

Rick's "studio" was in a semi-posh part of town with a lot of older warehouse buildings that had been renovated into lofts. His film company occupied several upper floors of one of these old refurbished buildings. I took the stairs five at a time as I raced up to the fourth floor where Rick said I would find her.

The scene I walked in on was massively fucked up. It was a movie set with a bedroom all lit up with studio lights, and a couple sitting on the bed, half-naked. The filming had stopped and they were both watching the commotion in the corner.

Two guys held down Sophia, who was screaming, "I can do this. Just give me a chance."

I ran at the guys, fully expecting to brutally murder them both, but as I neared, I realized they were not so much holding her down as they were trying to keep her shirt on her. She kept on trying to pull it up, and they were restraining her in order to prevent her from stripping.

"Sophia," I yelled, my voice demanding that she stop her crap, and she did. Taking in a breath, she looked up at me with wide eyes. "What the hell are you doing?"

The room went silent, and guys who'd been forcibly keeping her clothed backed away. When I made it to her and she still hadn't spoken, I knelt down in front of her, grabbed her arms, and looked into her eyes.

I lowered my voice and tried to calm myself. "Why are you here?" I stared into her eyes, which were seriously bloodshot, but she wouldn't meet my eyes as her gaze pinged around the room, apparently looking for an escape. "Sophia?"

She tried to turn away from me, but I still caught the tears that were filling her eyes.

Thirty-Two

MacKenzie

I'd filled the tub with warm water and lavender essential oil and was trying to calm my nerves when the phone rang. I let it ring for a while, thinking I'd let it go to voice mail and check it later. But the ringing kept going and going, and then, when it finally did stop, it picked up again a few seconds later and started all over again.

I sighed. My phone was in the living room. Who would be calling me anyway? I went through my short mental list as I got up and grabbed my towel. Maybe it was my neighbor Soni. After the last incident with her grandson, I'd given her my number and told her to call me if he ever showed up again. Maybe it was her.

I picked up my pace and snatched the phone from the coffee table. "Hello."

"MacKenzie, I need you."

It wasn't Soni, but I knew the voice instantly. My heart danced. "Yes," I said.

"It's Sophia. I need to get her to treatment. Can you help? I'm not sure how to do this."

"Of course," I said. "I'll make some calls. Where are you?"

"We're on our way to your place. See you soon." He hung up.

The desperation in his voice caught me off guard. Ian needed me. Sweet relief washed over me. Even if I couldn't have him the way I wanted him, I was still a part of his world. I'd pushed him away, but some invisible thread had tied us together, at least for now. A sense of purpose pushed me into action and I got to work.

I switched on my computer, threw on some yoga pants and a T-shirt, and began typing.

Finding a rehab center with openings late at night wasn't an easy thing. Ian's family could afford to pay, which made things a little easier, but I still ended up calling a handful of places before finally talking one into taking her.

The downside was that the place was a full three-hour drive away.

Ian hadn't told me anything about the state Sophia was in, though I assumed she was high. When they arrived, I found I was right, although, thank God, she was going to treatment of her own free will.

"Three hours away. Isn't there somewhere closer?" he asked when I told him the news.

I shook my head. "It's hard to find a bed at one of these places at the last minute. Three hours isn't that bad. I can drive part of the way."

"No, I can't ask you to come. You found us a place. That's enough."

"Oh no, I'm going with you."

My firm gaze met his. *Sorry, buddy, there's no room for argument.* He couldn't possibly think it was a good idea to drive three hours alone with his coked-up sister. She needed a sitter.

He looked tired; I'd noticed it when he first came in. It was like he'd been fighting so long and so hard, he just didn't know if he had any more fight left in him. I hated seeing him like that.

I grabbed the backpack I'd packed while waiting for them to arrive and handed it to Sophia. "It's just a few things that might help." She looked at me curiously. "We're about the same size—T-shirts, yoga pants, underwear, and a toothbrush."

I shrugged as Ian watched me silently, his eyes tracking my every movement. Then I grabbed my purse and took Sophia's hand. "Come on. I want to do this for you. Please let me help."

Sophia was quiet, but pushed her arms through the straps of the backpack.

Ian led the way to his car. I sat in the back with Sophia and played as many car games as I could think of before switching to watching videos on Ian's tablet.

Occasionally I let myself glance up at Ian. I could see in his face that he was exhausted. He needed sleep. But every time I offered, he refused to let me drive. So I sat with Sophia and tried to keep her mood upbeat on the long ride.

We arrived at one in the morning. I'd never checked anyone in for treatment before, but I imagined it would take a ton of time. However, since she was willing to go, they hardly wanted us there at all. They needed Ian for his checkbook, but all the other paperwork could be filled out by Sophia since she was the consenting adult, and we were all but pushed back into Ian's car, and found ourselves back out on the road again by one fifteen.

We'd hardly had time to say good-bye to Sophia before they whisked her away. She'd hugged her brother and he'd whispered something that made her smile, then she'd walked away clutching the backpack I'd given her.

Ian let me drive on the way home. He tried to get me to listen to music, but I feigned a headache so we could leave it off in hopes that he would get some sleep. Thankfully he did fall asleep about a half hour into the ride back, leaving me awake with my thoughts.

Thirty-Three

MacKenzie

It was four a.m. when I finally pulled into Ian's garage. I found his usual parking spot and turned off the car. He lay back in the passenger seat, eyes closed, looking so peaceful as he slept.

I hated the idea of waking him and forcing him back into the reality of the situation, so I sat there, barely breathing, and let my eyes adjust to the dim light from the garage that crept in through the window, painting his face in shadows.

His straight nose, full lips, and the way his dark eyelashes rested against his cheeks was hypnotizing. Ian was the epitome of masculine beauty. His white T-shirt hugged him in a way that made his body seem even more godlike than usual. I licked my lips and admonished myself for wanting to trace my fingers over his chest.

"What?" he asked in a calm voice, snapping me out of my trance. He'd opened his eyes. The stillness must have woken him. He turned to face me, and the corners of his mouth tugged up playfully. "What are you looking at?"

I laughed. "Nothing. We're here."

His smile fell as the memory of the night's events came back to him. "You drove all the way? Why didn't you wake me?"

"You needed the sleep."

He looked around. "So why are we in my garage?"

"I thought I'd drop you here and catch a cab," I said.

He shook his head.

I shook my head back at him and shrugged. "What, are you going to drive me?"

He rubbed his hand over his head and sat up. "No, I don't like the idea of you going back to your neighborhood at this time of night."

"So, what? You want me to stay over tonight?" I raised my eyebrows at him and smiled.

"Actually, yeah. I do."

God, the idea of lying in bed with Ian was so enticing. Still, I'd already decided that Ian and I wouldn't happen. In fact, we couldn't happen if he wanted to fight in Vegas, something we both wanted desperately for him. Something he deserved.

"No," I said.

His brow furrowed. "I don't mean like that. I have a guest room." He took a deep breath. "I just don't want to worry about you tonight. It's been a rough day for me with all this Sophia stuff, and I'd feel a lot better if I knew you were safe. Call me old-fashioned, I don't care, but please humor me, just for tonight."

"Fine." I sighed. Honestly, I was too tired to argue, and after the drive to and from the treatment center, a cab ride home seemed too long of a wait to get to sleep.

He led the way to the underground ramp's elevator. The elevator walls were mirrored, of course, which meant that no matter how hard I tried to avoid noticing how delicious he looked in his just-tight-enough jeans, he was right there. The other alternative, looking up at his face, was something I knew I couldn't handle alone with him in the quiet elevator. I hazarded a peek, and his sleepy eyes were looking thoughtfully at me. I took a deep breath, folded my arms, and leaned back against the wall.

As he hit the button for his floor, I was reminded of the fact that I'd never actually been inside his condo. Every time I'd come over, we worked in his gym on the first floor, but his apartment was on the twenty-fourth floor. The top floor, of course.

When we got there, he led the way down the hall past several other units. At least he wasn't in one of those crazy penthouses where the elevator opened to his condo because the top floor was all his.

Ian's place was larger than mine, but still modest. It had a dark color scheme that was unquestionably masculine, from the deep cherry hardwood floors to the dark leather furniture, to the black appliances in the kitchen off the great room. But it was so tastefully done that I had my doubts as to whether he'd furnished it himself. It was elegant, but not enough so to keep my eyes from drifting back to his beautiful body. I was having a seriously hard time not looking at him in that white T-shirt.

"This place is so clean." I didn't mean to say it out loud, but apparently I was too tired to self-edit.

"Cleaners come once a week."

Duh, of course he didn't clean his own place. I stifled a laugh.

"Let me give you the quick tour." He took me down a hallway and showed me his small office, the guest bedroom, and guest bathroom. "This is you," he said, stepping inside.

The room was a decent size with a beautiful deep maroon theme. But it was so clean, it felt like a hotel room.

He headed over to a small dresser and opened the top drawer. "My sister used to crash here sometimes when she was in high school. I don't suppose this would fit you?"

He held up a shirt that had to be a size extra small, juniors. But I'd make it work.

"Sure. Thanks."

"There are new toothbrushes in the guest bathroom under the sink, and fresh towels in the closet if you want a shower or anything." As he said shower, his gaze drifted over my body, nothing subtle about it.

God, if I took a shower, would he join me? Delicious heat raced through me at the thought.

I caught myself biting my lip and turned away, pulling in a deep breath. "Thanks," I said again.

He lifted his hand and turned me back to face him, then cupped his rough palm against my cheek. "Thank you. I can't tell you how much I appreciated all your help tonight."

I was so tempted to cover his hand with mine and lean my cheek into it. It took every ounce of willpower I had, but I managed to nod and wait for him to reluctantly pull his hand away.

"I'm just at the end of the hall if you need anything. Good night." He closed the door behind him, and his footsteps padded down the hall.

I stood there for a moment, staring at the closed door to my room. Like an idiot, I was hoping for the world's oldest cliché. I wanted to stand on one side of the door while he stood outside it, each of us hoping the other would open the door so that we could collide into each other's arms and fall back onto the bed.

But stuff like that didn't happen to girls like me.

I turned away and pulled the covers down on the guest bed, then climbed in. I was so mentally and physically exhausted that I was sure I would get right to sleep. So sure that when an hour had passed and I was still awake, I was seriously amazed.

As I stared at the ceiling, I thought I heard footsteps coming toward my room, but I was so tired, I could have imagined it. Still, a desperate need bubbled up inside me, making me feel crazy. I had to know if he was there, if he still felt the same way about me as I did about him.

So I got up, took a deep breath, and pulled open the door. I was so shocked to see Ian standing directly in front of me, I stumbled a step back as he smirked happily at me.

"I couldn't…" I started as he interrupted me with, "I wanted…"

We both fell into an easy laughter, and I motioned for him to go ahead.

Ian rubbed a hand across the back of his neck. "I wanted to thank you for tonight. Again. I'm sorry I got you involved in all this, I just didn't know who else to call."

I nodded. "Ian, don't worry about it. I'm glad you called. I can't imagine you trying to do this all on your own." His small smile of gratitude was all the thanks I needed.

"What were you going to say before I interrupted?" he asked.

I shuffled my feet on the carpeting, digging my big toe into the plush fibers. "I couldn't sleep," I admitted.

He nodded. "Me neither. I'm glad you're here with me. Tonight was interesting, to say the least."

I watched his lips as he spoke, remembering how firm and soft they were at the same time. Then I mentally chastised myself for thinking about kissing him when he was clearly upset over his sister.

"But Sophia's tough. She'll fare okay," he added, his posture relaxing as he leaned back against the wall.

Okay, so maybe he wasn't that torn up after all. Sophia was a big girl, and she was now in the best possible place she could be. We had to stay positive and hope for the best.

"The truth is," he continued, "it's not easy to sleep knowing there's a beautiful woman just down the hall. I couldn't live with myself if I didn't at least try…"

His honesty surprised me. As his words hung in the space between us, Ian brought his hand to my cheek, lightly caressing my skin.

His touch awakened a need in me, one I'd been desperate to suppress, and I leaned into his warm palm. His touch felt so good, so right, that I struggled to comprehend why I'd been holding myself back from this for so long. I stepped closer.

His gaze moved between my lips and my eyes. "What about Chris?"

"What about him?"

"He's your boyfriend, MacKenzie. Shouldn't he be the one taking care of your needs?" His thumb brushed lightly along my cheekbone, making me dizzy.

I shook my head, my bold gaze not straying from his. If only he knew the truth.

"Not getting enough from Chris?" Ian's smirk was playful, but his words cut straight through me.

"We haven't...we're not..."

Oh dear God, someone please shut me up.

"Wait a second." His brow crinkled. "You're not fucking him?"

I flinched at his words, which came out harsh, like an accusation. "No."

"Why the fuck not?" He straightened, and his hand dropped away from me.

I shrugged. "It hasn't felt right."

I don't want Chris.

"And this?" He motioned between us.

Once again, my gaze latched onto his and refused to wander.

I want you.

As wrong as it was, I couldn't flat-out lie to him again. I needed to try to deny it and push him away, but the words refused to form in my mouth.

"Fuck it."

Ian curled a rough palm around the back of my neck and guided my mouth to his. His lips barely brushed against mine. His overt strength took a back seat, and the gentleness of his touch surprised me. Ian's hot breath whispered across my skin, causing little tingles of heat to crackle along my skin and down my spine, pooling low in my belly.

A tiny whimper escaped my throat. I needed more. When his tongue lightly brushed against my lower lip, I opened for him. His tongue flicked along mine, dampening my panties and sweeping away all my good sense.

Sweet memories of his tender kisses and sure, strong hands lifting me flooded my senses. The reverence in his hooded eyes as he drank me in lashed back at me from my subconscious. Blood rushed through my veins, and I was overwhelmed with the need to give in. But years of faking inner strength rose to the surface and I pulled a deep, shaky breath into my lungs, forcing myself to let it all go.

Ian wasn't the type to make a commitment— fighting came first. And I liked him enough that I wouldn't get in the way of his chance to break into the pros.

"Ian..." I breathed his name, and his lips broke from mine. "We can't," I whispered weakly.

He nodded.

"Not right now," I explained. "You can't lose focus on your fight."

His eyes danced on mine. "But after?"

Everything inside me screamed *yes*. But I sucked my lower lip into my mouth to avoid saying something stupid.

He nodded, and I thought I saw hope in his eyes.

A silent promise hung heavily in the air between us, and I knew we were both thinking the same thing. We couldn't ignore this explosive chemistry between us forever.

"This isn't over," he said, his tone direct and sure.

I stood there motionless as he swiped his thumb across my bottom lip in a tender gesture, then turned away and disappeared into his bedroom.

Holy fuck! I returned to the guest bedroom on shaky legs, my soaked panties and racing heart reminding me of the very dangerous game I was playing.

Thirty-Four

Kenzie was making me lose my fucking shit.

She could be so sweet. The way she stepped in and found the place for Sophia, even going so far as to pack a bag for her and insist on coming along for the drive to the treatment center. And then later at my place, when she let me hold her and pull her in for the kiss, it felt so right that I was sure she felt it too. Her sweet taste and the hunger in her eyes when she looked at me, those were the memories that played in my head as I finally fell asleep.

It wasn't until the next morning that I really thought about what she'd said. *Not right now.*

Why the fuck not? Sure, she thought she was a distraction, but being away from her was so much worse. I got up, threw on some shorts, and marched back down the hall to the guest bedroom to confront her. I was going to make her understand. We didn't have to wait.

But the door hung open, the bed was made, and she was gone. Not even a hint remained that she'd ever been here.

When I got to the gym, MacKenzie was there, but she was never alone. If she wasn't talking with one of the guys, Chris was hovering somewhere nearby.

During our afternoon session, Chris seemed to be watching us the whole time. That, and she had me doing my exercises within earshot of several of the other guys, which made talking to her impossible. What really fucked me up, though, was how cold she'd become. It was such a complete turnaround from the way she'd been the night before, it was driving me nuts.

"Three sets of twelve with the sixties, please." Her voice was monotone. She pointed at the weight, refusing to look me in the eyes.

I bent down into her line of vision as I picked up the weight and tried to catch her eye, but she averted her gaze again.

Son of a bitch.

Behind her, Chris headed into his office. We were just out of sight of the one-way mirror, so I took advantage of the opportunity, shelved the weight, threw Kenzie over my shoulder, and headed out back to the alley.

"Ian, put me down," she demanded. "What are you doing?" She twisted and squirmed, trying to get me to release her, but she was so small I could easily maintain control. Her attempts were futile. I was going to get her alone to talk to her, whether she wanted to or not.

"We need to talk," I said as I kicked open the back door and stepped outside.

"You can't do this, it's kidnapping. Let me go," she said, her voice filled with irritation.

I headed a bit farther down the alleyway before finally setting her feet on the ground.

She straightened out her clothes, then put her hands on her hips. Her gaze darted briefly to mine, then she focused her hateful glare at the wall behind me. "There's nothing to talk about."

"Don't give me that. There's something between us. You feel it; I know you do. Last night you said you just wanted to wait until my fight was over, but I don't want to wait. Because waiting for you is a worse distraction than being with you could ever be. Break up with Chris. I don't care what he does. He can beat the crap out of me. You don't like him; you don't even want to fuck him." I paused, taking a deep breath to calm myself. "But you and I both know that's not the case with me. You want me. I see it in your eyes."

MacKenzie looked down at the ground and shook her head. "No, I don't." Her response was almost a whisper, but her words stung.

She couldn't mean them. I stepped closer and lifted her chin. Her eyes darted around, only meeting mine briefly. What was she hiding?

"Bullshit," I said, barely keeping my voice under control. "What's changed?"

"What?"

"You heard me. What's changed? Last night when I kissed you, you kissed back. You said we had to wait until my fight was over. Now I'm saying I don't want to wait. I *can't* wait. I need you now. And you won't even look me in the eye. So, what has changed?"

"Ian, I'm sorry about last night. I wish it hadn't happened that way, but you have to remember, I was exhausted. We'd been driving all night, and I just wasn't thinking clearly." Her eyes lifted to mine, and they were filled with pain.

I shook my head. "I don't believe you."

"It's the truth. I want to be with Chris, and you have to let me. I was weak last night. I slipped. It won't happen again."

"But why?" God, if she really did want to be with him, of course I would let her, but I couldn't see it. There was no way he was right for her.

"Chris is a good guy. He's someone…" MacKenzie paused and swallowed. "Someone who would stick around, and make a good husband one day." She looked away, then dropped her gaze to the ground.

I rubbed my hand over my hair. What she said almost made sense, but I wasn't buying it.

"You want me." I closed the distance between us, cupped her face in my hands, and kissed her lips gently. She didn't pull away, but she didn't kiss me back either. Instead, a small sob escaped, and I pulled away to see tears escaping her closed eyes.

Shit. What the fuck was I doing? I didn't want this. I didn't want to hurt this girl. Not ever.

I took a step back and lifted my hands in apology. "I'm sorry."

"I don't…" MacKenzie's voice shook, and she took a breath. "I don't think you need our sessions anymore. Your shoulder is fully healed. You've been fighting at full strength for a week now."

She swallowed, wiped her eyes, then turned and headed down the alley.

Thirty-Five

I was one serious basket case. I hated myself so much it made me sick.

Falling into Ian's arms that night felt so right, but it was such a stupid thing to do. And so weak. I'd slipped up, almost letting him know how I felt, opening the door for him to get distracted. He was so agitated, I thought he would march right into the gym and tell Chris about us. But if he'd done that, Chris surely would have pulled him from the fight.

Ian had been cleared by the doctor to start sparring again, but Chris still wasn't sure he'd be ready. That morning he informed me that he'd arranged for Jonah to come with us to Vegas, just in case he had to pull Ian from the fight.

I couldn't have that.

Which was why I needed to be strong. If Ian couldn't keep the distance between us in the week and a half leading up to the fight, I would have to be the one to take care of it. I didn't like having to stop our physical therapy sessions, but I could no longer trust myself with him. And in all honesty, he was back to full strength. We could have stopped working together several days before, but I was too selfish. I wanted more time with him.

That had to stop.

So when I left him in the alley, I went back inside, cleaned myself up in the bathroom, and headed to the office to find Chris. On my way across the gym, Blondie, the girl I'd seen him with the other day, was exiting the office.

She saw me and changed course to intercept me, then paused next to me. "You may think Chris is yours but, honey, he's been having his meals elsewhere. Soon enough, he'll be mine." Once she'd dropped her little bombshell, she smirked and continued the rest of the way to the front door.

Too bad for her that her threat didn't have the intended reaction. My heart belonged to someone else, so it was only fitting that Chris's did too.

I was so busy watching Blondie's exit that I bumped right into Chris. "*Oof.* Sorry," I said.

"Hey, babe. How did physical therapy go? Was Ian cooperative today?"

"Fine," I said. "He's doing really well. So well, in fact, that he graduated. He doesn't have to do those exercises anymore. He can use the time to focus on other things."

At that moment, Ian walked back in the front door of the gym. When his eyes found Chris and me, he looked away and lifted a hand to knead the back of his neck.

Obviously he felt responsible for making me cry. I hated that he felt that way, but there was nothing I could do to change it. He needed to think we were over, and that there was no chance of us ever happening. He needed to focus on healing and his fight in Vegas. Besides, we'd never work anyhow, and I'd end up with even more of a broken heart than I had now.

I slipped my hand into Chris's and got up on my tiptoes, giving him a peck on the cheek, then glanced over to make sure Ian was watching. By the way his jaw tightened, it was safe to assume he was definitely watching.

Chris turned to face me and gave me a wet kiss on the lips. "I thought you didn't like PDA at work. What was that for?" He smiled.

I forced myself to smile back.

IAN

Apparently Kenzie never told Chris about the night she spent in my guest room. I knew this because Chris didn't beat me senseless the next day, the way he probably should have for trying to move on his girl. The cold shoulder I received from Kenzie through the rest of my training leading up to the fight was so much worse. I would have taken a beating from Chris if it meant I could have stolen another moment with Kenzie. But she made it clear with her emotionless stares that we were done.

Her devotion to Chris was making me insane. How could she want to be with someone she wasn't even sure she wanted to fuck? That day at my home gym, when I had her folded in half, wet as fuck and begging for it, kept resurfacing in my mind. She'd been mine for the taking, offering herself to me.

What had she said about Chris? *It hasn't felt right.* But for some insane reason, she refused to give up on him, on them.

Watching her with someone else, even if it was someone she chose, did things to me. Every time Chris kissed her, I punched harder, kicked faster, and pushed myself further than I had before. Maybe the only benefit of her refusing to be with me was that I was redoubling my training effort.

The thought of Kenzie, my Kenzie, with someone else tormented me. It filled me with an overwhelming rage that I could only relieve by pounding, ripping, and kicking the shit out of my sparring partners. And they were feeling it; I could see it in their eyes, the fear. The smaller guys wouldn't work with me, so I was left with Jonah and several guys in the weight class above me. Even Jonah was getting bruised in practice. But he loved the fight so much, he would shake it off and come back for more. He and Chris worked with me all day on different moves and last-minute techniques.

When I went home, I threw myself into watching and re-watching my opponent's old fights. I ate, breathed, and crapped fight videos. I was sick of watching the same fights over and over; I had them memorized. I knew all his moves. But I continued to watch them in the odd chance I would see something new I hadn't seen the first eighty times I'd watched them. That, and they were the only way to stifle thoughts of Kenzie.

It was only through my dedication to the fight that I made it through the next week and a half without her. When the fight was over, I wasn't sure how I'd fucking deal.

Thirty-Six

The next ten days were hard. I tried to stay away from Ian, but he was training at the gym all the time, and I still needed my paycheck to make rent, so I couldn't leave. Instead, I tried to make sure he saw me with Chris as much as possible.

I'd been worried Chris would take my new affection and try to push our relationship to the next level. Thankfully, he had too much to do. If he wasn't coaching Ian, he was on the phone with sponsors or the fight organization, working on all the last-minute details. I made sure to constantly point out how much stronger Ian had gotten, and that he was more than ready to win.

Still there was one part of fight preparation that worried the crap out of me—cutting weight. Before the fight, Ian had to reduce his weight by twenty pounds, which was something all the fighters did. But they did it in such a short amount of time that it made the nurse in me cringe, and the part of me that cared for Ian want to cry.

I had to sit back and watch as he sweated and dehydrated himself the last few days leading up to the fight so that he would be able to hit the correct weight for his fighting class at weigh-in.

By the time we boarded the plane, he was so shaky that Jonah had to help him put his luggage in the overhead bin. My eyes fixed on Ian as he grabbed the back of the seat in front of him and slowly lowered himself into the aisle seat.

"He'll be fine, sweetie," Chris said, pulling my attention away. "He's been through this before." He chuckled as if it was no big deal, but I had a bitter taste in my mouth and my stomach was all cramped up. "You don't mind if I take the window seat, do you?" he asked. "It's easier for me to sleep on that side, and I want to try to get a nap in on the flight." He slid in, taking the seat without waiting for me to respond.

I sighed and shook my head. It was my first time on a plane, and I would have liked to see what it was like taking off, but I didn't feel like arguing. Besides, Chris was paying for the trip. I had set aside a few hundred dollars for spending cash, but wouldn't be here if he hadn't paid for my airfare and hotel.

I took the aisle seat next to Chris, and he lifted up the armrest between us. Putting his arm around me, he pulled me close. "Sorry I haven't been able to spend more time with you, Kenzie." He kissed me. "I promise we'll be able to spend more time together once we get Ian all set up for the fight."

He folded me into his arms, forcing my head into his shoulder, which was drenched in cologne. My almost constant stress headache worsened and my stomach, which had been acting up for the past several weeks, gurgled. It would be a long flight.

It wasn't until the plane had taken off, and Chris pulled the window shade to get some sleep, that I was finally able to free myself from his grasp. When the seatbelt sign pinged off, I got up and headed for the bathroom. Not just to get away from Chris, but because my stomach issues were threatening to turn the corner after the roller coaster of emotion combined with the motion of the plane at takeoff.

I made it to the bathroom just in time. Latching the door, I flipped the seat up on the toilet, pulled my hair back, and let my lunch back out the same way it had come in.

Afterward, I washed my face in the small sink and looked at myself in the mirror. I was a mess. My face was pale and my hair was a gnarl-fest. I ran my fingers through my hair and consoled myself. At least now I wouldn't be lying to Chris when I told him I was too sick to go out tonight.

I frowned. The fight was the day after tomorrow. I just needed to make it through two more days, then

I could be done with this whole mess. I could break up with Chris, find a new job, and forget about the man who'd stolen my heart.

Love was too dangerous a game. I'd known that my entire life, but somehow these last few months, I'd forgotten it. I needed to be strong.

I pulled the latch on the door and slid it open, and was shocked to find Ian standing just outside.

"I saw you rush back here. Are you okay?"

Fully aware that I'd just thrown up and had no access to a toothbrush, I covered my mouth. "I'm fine," I said through my fingers.

"You don't look fine," he said, pulling my hand away from my face so that he could see. "You're pale." His gaze darted down the aisle to our seats, then he put his hand on my shoulder. "Just sit down for a minute." He guided me to an open seat a few rows down, and squatted next to me.

I hadn't felt dizzy, but sitting down felt really good just then. I might have been a little woozy. "I'm fine," I protested. Because even if I wasn't, Ian didn't need to know. We'd been doing a good job of staying apart so far. No need to ruin that now. I was so close to the finish line.

He brushed my hair back behind my ear, making a shiver rush down my face and neck. But then the plane hit a bit of turbulence, and he stumbled and grabbed the seat's back for support. His arm shook, reminding me of the frail state he was in.

"Don't worry about me," I said. "You should be resting. You're the one who's all dehydrated." I stood up and tried to make him take the same seat I'd just vacated.

"Nonsense," he said.

"Look at you, you're shaking. I…" My voice wavered. "You need water."

"Kenzie." His voice was calm and soothing, and he once again put a hand on my shoulder. "If I don't make the correct weight, I can't fight. You know that. Besides, I do this before all the fights. I'll be fine."

I looked at him again. He was still the same tall, strong Ian I'd always known. Despite that, something about his posture made me wanted to take him in my arms and hold him. I wanted to care for him while he went through this insane bit of self-torture, but I couldn't. I needed to be strong, so I balled up my fists.

"Fine," I said. "But don't waste your energy worrying about me." My voice came out harsh. Ian needed to focus on his fight, not me.

I turned away and headed back down the aisle. I wanted him to have his fight, and I wanted him to win. All this self-sacrifice couldn't be for nothing.

IAN

I'd been to Vegas countless times before, often enough to see fights, but this was the first time I was going to be the one in the cage. I was so pumped, my heart felt like it beat triple-time on the flight there. That combined with the physical strain of sweating and avoiding liquids to cut weight made me a total wreck.

Still, I seemed to be the only one who noticed when Kenzie ran off to the restroom as soon as the seatbelt sign was turned off. Both Chris and Jonah had managed to pass out, so even though I'd been getting the stink-eye from Kenzie for the past week—ever since I confronted her—I went back to check on her.

She'd looked frail and delicate. So much so that it took everything in me to not fold her in my arms and hold her. Of course, she denied anything was wrong and tried to turn it around on me, making it about my health. That was so like her. She wouldn't let me help, and turned away from me, storming back to her seat.

After everything we'd been through, I still wanted her. I knew we were meant to be together, but she was wearing me down, so I'd promised myself to not think about it until after the fight. A promise I definitely could not keep.

It was midnight local time when we landed. Still, when we got to the hotel, I was nowhere near tired.

"This way," Chris said as the elevator doors opened to our floor. Chris led the way with his luggage and Kenzie followed him, wheeling her small suitcase.

"Are you sure I can't carry that for you, Kenzie?" I asked.

I'd offered to carry it for her earlier, but Chris had given me a weird, almost bitter look. I wasn't sure how he could be mad if he wasn't going to man up and help out his girlfriend. I swear, if he didn't start being more attentive to Kenzie, I would punch him.

"No, it's fine. I've got it." She smiled politely.

"This is us," Chris said. He slid in the key card and opened the door.

I hadn't intended to eavesdrop, but my room was only a few doors down. As I searched my pockets for my own key card, I could hear them talking.

"This is my room?" MacKenzie said.

My pulse quickened. Were they staying in separate rooms?

"This is our suite," Chris said.

Deflated, I located my key card and was about to let myself in when I heard Kenzie say, "I thought you said I would get my own room."

I put my key card back in my pocket and pretended to continue to search. Did she really demand separate rooms? My heart pounded with my elevated pulse. If she wasn't going to fuck him, why the hell was she still with him?

"Don't worry, my little Kenzie," Chris said. "I didn't forget our deal. You have your own room."

"But you just said—"

"This is our suite. My bedroom is on one side, and yours is—"

The door closed behind them and I could no longer hear. But I'd heard enough. This whole time Kenzie had been giving me the cold shoulder and making me think she was getting closer to Chris. But it was a load of shit. They still hadn't fucked.

Maybe there was still hope for us after all.

Just how the fuck was I supposed to focus on the fight?

Thirty-Seven

MacKenzie

As we headed up to our floor in the hotel elevator, I started to feel sick again. Being with Chris was wearing on me. Big-time.

The unsettled feeling in my stomach only intensified when Chris showed me the rooming situation. "My bedroom is over there." He pointed at one of the doors that led off the front room of our suite. "And your bedroom is over there."

He smiled proudly as panic filled me. I could manage the next few days with Chris, going out on dates and putting him off. But I wasn't sure I could handle sharing a room with him. Which was why I thought we'd agreed on separate rooms.

"I…" I searched for words that wouldn't make me sound like I was freaking at the idea of being alone with him. "We…"

Crap. I couldn't find the words. I was so upset, but I didn't want him to get angry. He'd brought Jonah with us, almost as if he still wasn't sure that Ian was ready for the fight. He'd never said it again outright, but it still felt like Ian's participation in the fight somehow hinged on my staying with Chris. If I exploded on him now, he might just pull Ian.

"Okay," I said.

The living area of our suite had floor-to-ceiling mirrors on two walls, black faux-leather furniture, as well as black laminate-covered particleboard end tables. All that combined with the mini bar made the room scream *cheap stripper party.* Although this was Vegas, so make that *cheap hooker party.*

The thought made my skin crawl, and I suddenly wondered if I had enough energy to take a shower. I took a deep breath and headed over to check out my room. I slid the door open, noting that the room was tiny and only contained a bed and a small closet. I put my bag on the bed. At least there was no stripper pole.

Chris followed me and leaned against the doorway. "Get yourself settled and cleaned up, or whatever, then we'll go grab a drink at the bar."

"Chris, I don't feel well. I think I need to just crash," I said.

He looked at me. "Hmm. Yeah, I guess you don't look too good. It's late. We can always go out tomorrow."

"Sounds good."

Chris headed back toward his room, and I slid the door closed so that I could get ready for bed. There was no lock. Not that I didn't trust Chris, he was always a gentleman, but I needed a room that was just mine where I could lock out the rest of the world. One place that was safe from everything, and mine alone.

I didn't have that.

Two more nights. I could get through this.

Couldn't I?

Thirty-Eight

IAN

I was running on adrenaline and couldn't sleep at all that night. If I wasn't busy forcing thoughts of Kenzie out of my mind, I was rushing through fight scenarios. My brain absolutely refused to calm down enough to let me sleep.

The next day after weigh-in, I spent a good part of the evening rehydrating and carb-loading. Even after a huge meal, I still couldn't find sleep, so I met Chris, Kenzie, and Jonah for drinks at the bar. Hell, even if I couldn't drink, maybe I could catch a contact buzz.

At the bar, I felt instantly more at ease. It helped that Kenzie was looking better. She had some color in her cheeks, though part of that might have had to do with the fact that she was on her second glass of wine.

"How's your room?" I asked Chris.

"It's big," he said. "We'll need to throw you an after-party there when you win tomorrow." He put his arm around Kenzie when he said "we" as if he owned her.

Possessive bastard. I tried not to let it get to me, but my shoulders tensed. *She's mine.*

My eyes darted to Kenzie. She seemed sad, but she forced a smile when Chris looked at her, then took another sip of wine.

Chris flagged down a waitress. "Another round."

A hand grabbed my shoulder, making me jump and look behind me. A tall, slender woman with long dark hair and wearing a skintight little black dress looked down at me.

"Hello, handsome." Her hand trailed up my neck and lightly brushed through my hair. She stepped closer, arching her back so that her tits were only inches from my face.

Not subtle at all.

MacKenzie

There were prostitutes in my neighborhood back home. The bulk of them were addicts making money to feed their habit. The one who approached Ian was nothing like them. She was beautiful. Which shouldn't have bothered me; after all, I'd been pushing him away so long that he had to think I wasn't interested.

Still, I didn't like anyone propositioning Ian. It made me so upset that I might have increased my wine consumption just a bit.

Ian looked up at her when she approached. "Hi," he said in a low voice.

"You guys wanna party?" she asked.

Ian looked over at me. He seemed to be considering something, but I couldn't read the look on his face. Finally, he turned back to her. "Sorry, not interested."

She turned to Jonah. "I could find a friend if you wanna double-date."

Jonah smiled, but didn't say anything.

Next she turned to me. I was unable to hide my disapproval of her lifestyle choice, and she could see it in my face. She smirked at me and said, "Or we could all party if your girl here wants to join in." Her gaze drifted to Chris.

I thought for a second that Chris was considering it, but he also said nothing.

"We're not interested," Ian said, his voice still low.

"You sure, honey? Because I'd give you a good deal." Her focus flowed down Ian's body as if undressing him with her eyes. I fought the urge to tell her to back off.

Ian smiled and shook his head. "Like I said. Not interested."

She gave Ian one last look before chuckling to herself and walking away.

Chris watched her go. "You and your no-sex rule." He shook his head. "You know it's not proven that abstinence makes you a better fighter."

I looked at Ian, wondering if what Chris was saying was true. I'd just assumed it was.

Ian took a swig of his water. "It hasn't been disproven either. The no-sex thing works for me. That's all that matters."

Chris smiled. "I'm just saying, maybe you should have asked her how much the discount was before you sent her away."

Ian forced a smile. He took a deep breath, finished his bottle of water, and said, "Well, guys, I think that's it for me. I've gotta try to get some fuckin' sleep."

"Me too," Jonah said, finishing off his beer in one gulp. "I'll head up with you."

I finished off my second glass of wine and ordered another. Chris and I spent another hour or so in the bar, and by the time we got up to head back to our room, I was definitely buzzed.

Buzzed enough to let Chris slip his arms around my waist and hold me close to him in the elevator. I let my head rest on his chest as we went up in silence. When the elevator pinged on our floor, I realized I'd been imagining Chris was Ian. Something which made me laugh for no apparent reason.

"What's so funny?" Chris said as we headed down the hall. He stopped suddenly. "Oh, damn. Is that the prostitute?" He laughed into his fist like he was trying to hold back.

I followed his gaze down the hall. Sure enough, Ian was standing at the door of his room wearing nothing but his boxers, handing the prostitute from the bar a wad of bills. Tears welled in my eyes and my pulse raced. What the…? No way.

The prostitute brushed her fingertips down his bare chest, then patted him on the cheek.

My feet didn't want to move, but Chris guided me to the door of our room. "Come on. They're both consenting adults." He pulled out the key card to our suite and opened the door.

I wanted to turn back, run down the hall, and demand that Ian tell me why. Why would he sleep with some prostitute after all we'd been through together, and after all the crap he'd said about the no-sex rule. Why was it okay now?

But I couldn't, because Chris was right. They were both consenting adults. The fact was, I had pushed Ian away. I had no right to the feelings of betrayal and pain that brewed inside me. Still, that didn't make it hurt any less. I wanted to curl into a ball and die. My heart had just been crushed.

I followed Chris into the room. As he went to the bar and poured me another glass of wine and himself a shot, I sat down on the couch, feeling dazed, and completely empty.

Chris handed me the wine and sat down, then put an arm around me and pulled me close. Realizing he was looking at me expectantly, I forced a relaxed expression and took a sip of my wine.

Although I was looking at Chris, in my mind I still saw Ian paying that woman. The one who possessively drew her hand down his bare chest. Anguish washed over me and filled me so completely that I became numb. I'd been waiting this whole time, putting Chris off, and kidding myself into thinking that once the fight was over, Ian would take me back. That we would be together, finally, in every sense of the word. But after seeing him with that woman, I knew I didn't mean anything to Ian.

It didn't matter anymore if I stayed away from Chris. In fact, maybe I should sleep with Chris. Maybe that was all I needed to make a clean break from Ian. Mulling it over, I took another sip of wine.

"It's so good to finally have you alone," he said.

Chris's breath smelled like mouthwash and whiskey. He looked into my eyes and, even though it didn't feel right, I told myself it didn't matter, so I tried to smile.

He leaned in and kissed me, his lips cold and wet, then rotated his tongue around mine the same way he always did. It was so practiced and desperate that it made me feel bad for him. There was no way I could get into it, but I resigned myself to trying to let go and just seeing what happened. Maybe it would help me forget.

He slid his hands to my breasts and grabbed them, squeezing them tightly. When his fingers dug painfully into me, I pulled back.

"Ouch," I said.

"Sorry."

He loosened his grasp a little, but it still felt all wrong. Not only was he awkward as sin, but he did absolutely nothing for me. There wasn't enough wine in the world to make sex with Chris good. It was something I might have worked with him on, if I actually liked him, but the truth was that I didn't. He'd been civil to me, but I wasn't attracted to him. And there was the little issue that he wasn't faithful to me.

Maybe I did need a way to make a clean break from Ian, but this wasn't it.

"Sorry, Chris. I'm not ready." I pulled away.

"Sure, you are. We've been dating for months now. I know you're no virgin." He grabbed my hips, pulling them toward his.

"Yes, but…" I tried to pull away, but he held me firm. "I'm not feeling well."

"You've been saying that for weeks." He leaned in again and kissed me as he pushed me back so that I was lying on the sofa. Fear rose up in me and I sobered up almost instantly. He grabbed my wrists and started pushing his way between my legs.

Shit, was this actually happening?

"No, Chris." My fight-or-flight instinct kicked in and I started struggling against him.

"Chill, Kenzie," he said. But he didn't let go of me, instead keeping me firmly pinned to the couch. His hands circled my wrists so tightly it hurt.

"I said no!" I continued to struggle but couldn't budge him off me, and tears welled up in my eyes. Chris had been a fighter, and I was no match for him.

The self-defense moves Ian and I had worked on came flooding back, and I instantly went to work twisting my body in the way Ian had shown me. Chris continued to hold my arms down, but I wedged my legs up between us and used the strength in my thighs to push him away just long enough to grab hold of his hands, raise my legs, and use his face as a kicking bag.

I kicked and kicked as hard as I could. I must have kicked him eight or nine times before he finally pulled away.

"You fucking bitch." Chris fell back on the floor, holding his nose.

Frantic, I jumped up from the couch and ran out of the suite, following the signs to the exit. I found the stairwell and started running down the stairs, taking them three at a time. My eyes blurred with tears, and I whimpered as I ran down several flights, then stopped short.

Where was I going? I couldn't stop crying, and there was no way I was going to walk through a casino hotel lobby, bawling my ass off.

I wanted to go home, but my wallet was in the room with Chris. Not that I had enough money in there to buy myself a plane ticket home. Of course, I could call Alexa and ask her to loan me the money, but my phone and her number were in the room with Chris.

Ian had his fight tomorrow so I didn't want to bother him, but short of sleeping in this stupid stairwell, it seemed like the only option. He had

Cade's number. I could get in touch with Alexa that way, and maybe I could still get out of here tonight.

I made my way back up the steps to our floor and silently crept down the hall to Ian's room. Although I'd managed to stop crying, my heart beat rapidly. I didn't like being back on the same floor with Chris.

As I knocked on Ian's door, I kept an eye on the door to the suite.

Thirty-Nine

IAN

Fuck!

I'd just started nodding off to sleep when someone knocked on my door. I lay in bed silently. Maybe if I ignored the first knock, they would go away. But then there was another, this one more frantic.

"What?" I growled as I shot up and stormed over to the door, not even bothering to look through the peephole, because whoever it was had knocked on the wrong damn door, and I was going to give them a piece of my mind. "Where's the fucking fi—"

I yanked open the door to find Kenzie, who'd obviously been crying. She shrank back from my rage.

Shit!

"Kenz, I'm sorry. What's wrong? Are you okay? Where's Chris?"

My mind raced as I scanned her from head to toe. She didn't look physically hurt, but her eyes were red and tear filled and her lips quivered, and she held herself so small as she shivered. She still wore the cute dress she'd worn earlier, but she was barefoot. Instantly I wanted to take her in my arms and protect her from whatever had happened.

But I knew better than to try to hold her again. She'd made it very clear that she wanted nothing to do with me. So instead I buried my intense need to hold her, took a deep breath, and asked, "Where are your shoes?"

She looked down at her feet slowly as if she hadn't realized she was barefoot. "They're with my phone and my wallet."

I didn't understand. "Did someone steal your wallet, phone, and shoes?"

"Can I come in, please?" Her voice was a shaky whisper.

I nodded and waved her inside, checking the hallway to make sure whoever or whatever had made her this way wasn't out there. Then I shut the door and guided her to the small seating area in my room.

"Where's Chris?" I asked again when we were both seated on the couch.

She shook her head but didn't say anything, instead looking at the floor. I searched her eyes for the strong Kenzie I knew, but she'd been ripped apart. My instincts to protect her were overwhelming. Every muscle in my body tensed. I would be kicking the shit out of someone, if she could just tell me what happened and who I was going to murder for making her look this broken.

I put my hands on her shoulders and made her look at me. "Listen, Kenzie. You're scaring me. I can't help you if you don't tell me what happened."

"Nothing," she whimpered, then fell into my arms and began to cry.

I wrapped my arms around her. It felt so right holding her in my arms—how could this possibly be wrong? I should be the one here for her. I held her gently and let her weep. Her breath mixed with tears warmed my bare chest, and my heart fucking ached for this woman. How could anyone hurt her?

Nothing happened? *Bullshit*. My mind raced through the possible scenarios, all of which ended with me murdering someone in cold blood.

"Are you hurt?" I asked.

"No." She kept her face buried in my chest.

I ran my hand gently over her soft hair, then realized I shouldn't and pulled my hand away. Chris should be holding her like this, comforting her. If that was who she really wanted to be with. Where the hell was he?

"Is Chris okay?"

She didn't answer right away. "I told you, nothing happened," she said to my chest.

Maybe that was it. Maybe she had finally broken it off with Chris. God, if that were true…

But I couldn't feel happy about that, not if breaking up with him hurt her this much. No, if that was what happened, it had destroyed her. And I could never be happy about that. Besides, I had no way of knowing what happened because she wouldn't fucking talk.

I sighed. I couldn't make her talk right now; she was too upset. So I held her and she cried softly in my arms for a while. When she'd finally calmed down, she pulled away and sat up.

"Sorry," she said. She wiped at her face, trying to remove the traces of tears, and I got her a tissue.

"Thanks." She dabbed at her eyes.

"Can I get you a water or anything?"

She nodded. "Can I borrow your phone?"

"Yeah." I grabbed her a bottle of water from the mini fridge and my phone from the nightstand, handing them both to her.

Kenzie scrolled through my phone. "I just need to call Cade and get Alexa's number, then I'll get out of your hair."

Forty

Damn it. I hadn't meant to fall apart like that in front of Ian. The plan was just to get in, use his phone, and get out. He had his big fight tomorrow, and for some reason, even after seeing him with that stupid hooker, I still wanted him to win.

But at the sight of him I completely fell apart. I couldn't hold it in. He was so strong, and the concern that filled his eyes was so real. I was selfish; I fell into him and let his strong arms hold me. Protect me. It wasn't just about Chris's unwelcome advances, it was everything, the deep loneliness that came from my past, the fact that I knew for certain Ian and I were through… It was all too much to process. I sat in his arms, crying, and felt safe from the destruction around me. I knew if I was with Ian, nothing like what had happened with Chris would ever happen to me again. I'd never have to worry about someone hurting me. Because Ian would protect me. He was safe.

So I fell into his arms and weakly wept against his bare chest, allowing myself to take the comfort he offered for a few minutes, until I was able to regain my composure—or what was left of it.

He lent me his phone, and I called Cade and got Alexa's number.

"Hello?" she answered. She was up, working an all-nighter at the hospital.

"Alexa. It's MacKenzie."

There was a pause. "Where are you calling from?"

"I'm in Vegas. Ian lent me his phone."

I glanced over to see Ian across the small room, sitting on his bed, watching me. Needing some privacy, I got up and went to his bathroom, shutting the door.

"I sort of need a favor," I said under my breath. "I need to get home, like now. Can you loan me the money for a plane ticket? Normally I wouldn't ask, but I promise I will pay you back."

"Wait, why don't you have your phone? Are you okay?"

"I'm fine." I paused, taking a deep breath. "Chris and I may have had a small…falling-out. I can't stay here with him. I have to get out of here."

"Oh God. I'm sorry, sweetie. Sure. I'll go online and buy you a ticket. Don't worry about the money. I just want to make sure you're okay. He didn't hurt you, did he?"

"No," I lied. Only my pride, my will, and my faith in humanity. Oh, and my boobs. "We just broke up."

"And where's your phone?" she asked.

Spanish inquisition, much?

"It's in Chris's room. I kinda stormed out, and I don't want to go back in. I thought I would ask Ian to get my stuff from him once the fight was over."

It was mostly true. I didn't like lying to Alexa, but the truth hurt too much. I wasn't ready to relive those horrible moments when I was alone with Chris and he tried to take everything away from me.

"Okay, sure," she said. "I'll find you a flight right now and call you back soon."

We hung up, and I sat down on the edge of the tub.

Ian knocked on the door. "Kenzie?"

"Yeah," I said.

"Everything okay?"

I got up and opened the door. No sense in hiding in his bathroom while I waited. "Yeah," I said. "Alexa's going to find me a flight home, then I can get out of your hair."

"You're going home?" He looked upset. Dang it, why was he upset that I was leaving? He was the one sleeping with prostitutes.

"What's wrong with that?" I asked.

He ran his hand through his hair. I caught his eyes glancing down my body. "I guess I was just hoping you would see the fight."

I wanted to see his fight too. More than he knew. I wanted to see him finally have his chance.

I shook my head. "I have to go. I don't have anywhere to sleep."

"You and Chris broke up." He tilted his head to the side and gave me a sympathetic look.

If only it were just that. If it were only that easy. I wanted to tell Ian the truth, and maybe, if he still cared about me, he would take me back. But if he knew what Chris had done—how he'd forced himself on me—he wouldn't let it go.

I'd seen how protective Ian was with his sister, and women in general. If I told him what Chris did, I had a feeling he would go after Chris. And that would not end well. It would definitely wreck him physically for his fight tomorrow. Besides, even if I did tell him the truth, would I ever be able to get him back? I had pushed him away so many times, there was no way.

"We broke up." I nodded, chewing on the inside of my cheek. That was one way of putting it.

"Stay here with me. I'll sleep on the couch. You can see the fight tomorrow, then get a flight after."

"Thank you, but no. I'm not putting you out like that. I want you to get your sleep. As soon as Alexa calls back, I'll be out of here."

Ian's phone rang. It was Alexa. "Sweetie, I have some bad news," she said. "There are no more flights out until tomorrow morning."

I felt my shoulders fall. "Crap." My mind raced to find something else I could do. "I'll go to the desk and see if they have any rooms left for the night."

"I already called them and tried that. Your hotel and all the ones nearby are fully booked. There's a bunch of conventions in town. Can you stay with Ian?"

I looked at Ian, who was watching me.

"What is it?" he asked.

I shook my head at him. "I can't. I won't put him out like that."

Ian jumped up and pulled the phone out of my hand. "What's up?" He listened while Alexa filled him in on the situation, then said, "Yeah. She can stay here. I don't want her running off to some suburban motel in the middle of the night. I'd feel better if she stayed here."

He handed the phone back to me. "It's settled." His look said there was no talking him out of it.

I put the phone back up to my ear. "I guess I'm staying here."

"Look, there's no reason you can't stay for the fight. Cade and I are arriving tomorrow. I'll text you our flight info and you can meet us at the airport. You can stay with us and come home after."

I watched Ian as he pulled an extra blanket and pillow out of the closet and started setting up on the couch. He was still in just his boxers, and at the sight of his muscular arms, legs, and back, I licked my lips. His brow furrowed as if he was thinking about something. God, I wanted to watch his fight.

"We'll see," I said.

Forty-One

IAN

Kenzie hung up the phone. "You better be making up the couch for me," she said. Her hands on her hips and bossy tone made me smile. She was so cute when she was demanding.

"Nope, I'm taking the couch."

"Ian, you need your sleep," she pleaded. Her eyes begged me. Saying no to her was nearly impossible, but there was no way she was sleeping on that couch. I wasn't fucking raised that way.

"How the hell am I going to sleep knowing you're uncomfortable?" I sat on the couch, laying claim.

She glanced at the bed, then back at me. "But I don't want to sleep in your bed. The couch will be much more comfortable for me."

I laughed. "Kenzie, there's no way you're getting out of this. Get in bed."

"Ian, I really don't want to." She looked away from me, her face pinched as if she were worried, so I got up and went over to her.

"What's going on?"

She turned her head away and bit her lip, her face turning red. "I don't want to say."

I rolled my eyes. "Kenzie, if you won't say, then you don't get out of it. Lay down."

"But..." She looked at the bed, almost disgusted. "Is that where you slept with her?"

My mind was reeling, trying to figure out what the hell she was talking about. I sat down on the bed. "Slept with who?"

"The prostitute," she almost whispered.

"Why would you think I slept with a prostitute?" I ran my hand across the back of my neck.

"I saw her at your door." She still looked at her feet, digging her toe into the carpet.

"You mean the one from the bar?" And then it all made sense. I took her hands. "It's the oldest trick in the book. My opponent sent her to my room. He was trying to get me to have sex the night before the fight. But I didn't sleep with her."

"Then why did you pay her?" Her gaze darted up to mine.

I squeezed her hands. "I was paying her to go away. Do you really think after what I've been through to get here, after all the years of training, that I would throw it away for a ride with a prostitute?"

She looked down again. "I guess I thought maybe you were just lying about the whole no-sex thing. Chris said there's no proof that it actually works."

I blew out a breath. This was Kenzie at her core; she didn't feel like she could trust anyone. Fuck, she might not even know how to trust people. I needed her to know that she could trust me.

"Kenzie, I would never lie to you. Never." I nudged her chin up so that she looked at me. "You are too important. I would never hurt you."

She nodded and let out a deep breath. "Okay."

"So will you please get in bed so that I can get some sleep before the fight tomorrow?" I asked.

"But I really don't want to take your bed."

"Will you at least sleep in it with me?" I knew what it sounded like, but I was so tired, and I just needed her to be safe and comfortable. "It's a big bed. I promise not to touch you."

Kenzie nodded.

I looked at the tight dress she was still wearing from earlier this evening. It hugged all her curves, and of course it was cut low. My dick stirred and I got up.

"I'll grab you a T-shirt."

Forty-Two

I changed into Ian's T-shirt and got in bed opposite him. "Good night," I said.

"'Night." He switched off the light.

I rolled onto my side, facing him. I couldn't see him because my eyes hadn't adjusted to the dark yet, but just knowing he was there made me feel safe. How was it that I couldn't stand the thought of sharing a suite with Chris, but with Ian in the same bed, I knew it would all be okay?

Ian's silhouette slowly came into view. He was lying on his side; I could tell from the bulging arm muscles that outlined his form. As my eyes adjusted, I took in his finely sculpted frame, his chest and his abs.

Oh, how I wanted him. Every piece of me wanted every bit of him. I wanted to run my fingers over every inch of his solid chest and eight-pack abs. I wanted to run my hot tongue down his body. I wanted to make him come apart the way he'd done to me on the mat in his gym. My panties got wet just remembering that day. His hot mouth on me, his fingers thrusting inside me.

No matter how much I wanted him, there was no way I would act on my desires. Not now. I'd already disrupted the crap out of him the night before his big fight. There was no way I would even try to tempt him to break his no-sex rule. This would be the one thing I could do right for him.

I took a deep breath and my eyes finally adjusted enough that Ian came into focus. Three feet away, facing me. Eyes open. We lay there, lost in each other's eyes, just a pillow's width away.

Finally, I pulled my hand out from under the sheets and held it open between us. An invitation. He took it and folded it in his own. Comforted, I closed my eyes. Because as long as I felt his strong, calloused hand around mine, I knew he was close by and I would be safe.

We lay there that way, just holding hands, until sleep took over.

****

The next morning when I awoke, Ian was still holding my hand, although he was asleep. The sheets had fallen away from him, and his broad chest lay bare. I was tempted to lie there and just watch him sleep, but he had a fight to win, and I had to figure out how to get my shoes and wallet from Chris. I needed cab fare to the airport, and my driver's license to get through security.

I went into the bathroom and changed back into my clothes from the night before. When I came out, Ian was awake, stirring in bed.

"'Morning," he said, smiling big as he stretched. "How'd you sleep?"

"Great. You?"

"Like a bear in winter." He was in a good mood. It had been a while since I'd seen him smile. It made me feel warm inside. But as soon as I started to enjoy it, his smile faded. "What happened to your arms?"

I looked down. I hadn't noticed, but my arms were covered in bruises. *Damn.*

I reached to cover them. "I don't know. I must have done something in my sleep."

It was the only thing I could think to say, because I knew exactly where the bruises were from. They were from Chris. But there was no way I was going to start something between Ian and Chris the day of the fight.

Ian leaped out of bed and took my arms in his hands, examining them. His face was stern, and his jaw tightened. "You didn't do this in your sleep,

MacKenzie. Don't lie to me. Why can't you just tell me what happened? Who did this to you?" The muscles in his neck tensed.

"No. I won't tell you," I barked. "I'm not here to be your distraction. You don't need to worry about me. Ian, pull it together and focus on your fight. I'm not your problem." I headed for the door.

"Kenzie, wait."

I pulled the door open and stepped out, stumbling on my bag, which had been placed right outside the door. Chris must have put it there. I pulled out the handle and started wheeling it to the elevator.

"Kenzie," he shouted down the hall after me.

I hit the DOWN button on the elevator, then turned to him. "Ian, a while back you promised me that you would win this fight. I've got my stuff, and Alexa will make sure I get home. You make sure you don't break that promise you made to me. You win your fight." The door to the elevator opened and I stepped inside.

The truth of my words hit me as the doors closed. I was a distraction to Ian. That was all I was, and all I would ever be. As long as I was around, he'd be unable to see his dream fulfilled.

I didn't want to be the one standing between him and his dream. I cared about him too much.

Forty-Three

IAN

Kenzie was gone. I couldn't believe she was fucking gone. As much as I wanted to curl her body next to mine and spoon her all last night, I could tell she needed space. It was written in the tearstains on her face.

Still I'd assumed, after what we'd been through together, that she would end up with me. I let myself believe that when she held my hand last night. But she'd marched out like she couldn't wait to leave. She was done with me. Wasn't even going to stick around long enough to see the fight, the fight I'd been prepping for my whole life. I thought she knew how much it meant to me. How much *she* meant to me.

The fight. That was how I would get through this. Focus all my energy on the fight. It had to be that, because after losing Kenzie, fighting was the only thing left, and it was time to get ready.

Chris wasn't in his room and wouldn't respond to any of my texts, but I found Jonah and spent the time leading up to the fight talking strategy and trying to keep myself calm enough to not fucking puke.

Strangely enough, the closer it got to fight time, the calmer I got. It made no sense, but this was how my nerves misbehaved before a fight. They peaked the day of the fight, but by the time I stepped into the ring, my mind was in a state of ass-kicking Zen.

I was a little worried about Chris. I knew he could take care of himself, but I'd called and texted him, left a note for him on his door, and heard nothing.

As we headed backstage before the fight, I texted Cade. I knew he was in town for the fight, and if Chris wasn't going to be there, I needed another coach. I might be the only one in the ring fighting, but a large entourage on entry ramped up the intimidation factor.

Cade messaged me right back and said he'd meet me backstage. I thanked God that Jonah had come out with us. He would have to do the coaching for two, but if I could get Cade to at least enter with me and sit near the cage, my team would look impressive.

The dressing room was almost as big as my hotel room, with a table and chairs on one end and a little seating area. I supposed if I were the champ I would need all the space for my huge entourage, but today I just felt lucky to be here.

Jonah helped me tape my hands, then I started my pre-game ritual. *Clear my mind of everything, and get ready to pound this guy into nothing.* I hopped up and down on the balls of my feet. It was all about finding the right place between calm and *let's beat the shit out of someone.*

"Aaah," I yelled. Yeah, I was ready.

The door opened and Chris slipped in. My hopping instantly slowed at the sight of him. His face was mangled. His nose ballooned out, obviously broken, and he had a black eye.

Jonah met him near the door. "Chris, what the fuck happened?"

Chris smiled through a fat lip. "Nothing. You should see the other guy. Let's get you ready for the fight," he said to me.

I looked him over; something about him made me feel on edge. His eyes darted nervously around the room, and he laughed.

"You're gonna kill this guy, Ian," he said as he moved toward me. But he was acting wary, as if he was unsure about something.

"Chris…" I said.

His eyes shifted again. "What?" He folded his arms, which was when I noticed the long red scrapes on his arms. Defensive claw marks.

My face heated up as I flashed back to the fear in Kenzie's eyes last night when I found her at my hotel door. How she wouldn't talk about any of it. And all the bruises on her arms the next morning.

I was a fucking idiot. All the signs were right in front of my face, but I didn't see it.

"You," I choked out. I advanced on him, my blood rushing through me and roaring in my ears.

"What's going on?" Jonah asked, approaching us cautiously.

Chris began backing up. "Did that little slut tell you I forced myself on her? Because she was acting like she wanted it, and then all of a sudden she was kicking me. That girl is psycho."

And I saw red.

Forty-Four

MacKenzie

At least Chris had made sure I got my stuff back. When I met Alexa and Cade at the airport, Alexa's pity-filled face was a sight for my sore eyes.

"Sweetie," she said, greeting me with a long hug. "How are you?"

"Better now that you're here," I said. And I did feel better than I had in a while. I was finally done with Chris. And I had to admit that I'd slept really well last night.

Her gaze fell to my hands. "You brought your bag."

I nodded. "You're going to loan me the money to fly home."

I'd resolved to go home on the next flight, rather than stay for the fight. I'd been enough of a distraction for Ian already, and needed to get as far away as I could so that he could concentrate.

She shook her head. "Nope."

"No? You won't loan me money?"

"I won't have to. You're staying for the fight. Our room's a double. You'll spend the night with us, and leave with your normal ticket tomorrow."

"Alexa, I don't want to stay for the fight. I just want to go home."

What I really wanted was to run back to the casino and back into Ian's arms. But that option was off the table.

"No, you can't go home." Alexa put her arm around me and started pushing me toward the taxi stand. "You deserve to see Ian win this fight. You worked so hard with him. There's no way we're letting you miss this." She looked to Cade for support.

He nodded. "Sorry. Alexa's the boss." He followed us with their luggage in tow as Alexa nudged me to the first cab in the taxi line.

"Alexa, I'm bad luck for him. All I am to him is a reason to lose his concentration. I need to get out of his way so he can win this fight, and the one after that and the one after that. He doesn't need me there to distract him. He needs time alone to focus on his dream."

"Shut it," she said. Her tone was playful, but she meant what she said. "I'm not having you miss this. You can trade tickets with Cade and sit by me. That way Ian won't even know you're there. Our seats are up in nosebleed land."

I sighed.

The cab driver got out and started loading their suitcases in back. Cade pried my bag out of my hand, putting it in the trunk with the others, then got in on the far side. I was being forced back to the fight whether I wanted to go or not.

Alexa gave me a shove toward the door, and I got in. She followed, and I rode back to the casino, wedged between Alexa and Cade and somehow feeling like a prisoner.

"If he loses the fight because I'm there, I'm gonna be pissed," I said.

Alexa patted my arm. "Sure, sure."

Forty-Five

IAN

All I saw was red.

"You forced yourself on Kenzie," I growled.

Chris continued his slow creep away from me toward the exit, but Jonah moved carefully in my direction to intercept.

Chris snarled at me. "I told you, she was acting like she wanted it. I didn't do anything to her." He pointed at his mangled face. "That bitch did *this* to *me*."

I flew at him with hands outstretched and grabbed him by the throat, then took him down on his back, landing on him hard. He clawed at my hands as I squeezed his throat. His face turned bright red and his mouth flapped open as he struggled for air. He kicked frantically at me, at my legs and anything he could reach.

I felt his blows, but they didn't hurt. What hurt was that this guy, who had pretended to be my friend, had forced himself on the woman I loved. I wanted blood.

Chris's fists flew at my face and he hammered away, but I kept holding his neck. He didn't deserve to breathe the same air as her.

Arms came from behind and wrapped around my neck and pulled.

"Ian," Jonah shouted in my ear. "Don't fucking do this. Whatever it is he did, it's not worth going to jail, and it's not worth throwing away your career. Let him go."

Jonah tugged at me, trying to pull me off Chris, but I wouldn't let go. I couldn't. Not after what he'd done.

"This little shit deserves to die after what he's put Kenzie through," I growled.

"So you'll spend the rest of your life locked up away from her, just to pay back this one guy?"

I loosened my grip a little as I let Jonah's words sink in. Chris's punches were weaker and fewer; he was about to pass out.

Jonah continued. "Wouldn't it be better for her if you were out here so you could protect her from other slimeballs like him?"

I let go and allowed Jonah to pull me off Chris. Chris coughed and grabbed his throat, fighting to take in air while simultaneously scrambling backward to get away from me.

"I knew there was something going on between you two," Chris said. His voice came out rough. "I saw you with her in the car that morning after your doctor visit. You kissed her. What was that about, Ian?"

Shit. He was right; I was a total dick. Not that it made what he did okay, but I'd been after his girlfriend since day one. I was no kind of friend.

"Why the fuck didn't you say something?" I asked. "Confront me! Punch me! Why play like you never saw it?"

"Because if I'd confronted you, you would have still won. She still would have gone home with you."

"But she chose you."

"You still think that?" Chris laughed as he pulled himself back on his feet. "What a joke. When she came to break up with me that day, I knew what she was up to. I saw the fear in her eyes. I also saw how much she cared about you, how much she wanted you to fight here in Vegas." He shrugged. "All she needed was a little motivation to stay with me. I gave her that motivation."

His broad smile was begging me to punch him. What the hell had he done to her?

"I may have suggested that the only way I *wouldn't* pull you from the fight was if she and I were still together."

"No way." I didn't believe him. There was no way Kenzie would do that. Stay with someone for me?

He continued. "I suggested you might not recover from your injury soon enough. After that, she couldn't keep her slutty hands off me."

My fist flew at him, but he saw it too late. His eyes widened as my knuckles made contact with his jaw. His skull was thick, but I hit him fucking hard. He spun backward, landing on the floor, and his eyes fluttered closed. He was breathing, but he was out.

Good, because I couldn't listen to one more second of his bullshit lies. There was no way Kenzie would sell herself for anything. She was smarter than that. If he'd been blackmailing her, she would have told me. We would have figured it out.

My knuckles hurt. *Fuck.* I'd taped up my hands but didn't have my gloves on yet, and I had hit him really fucking hard.

Jonah glanced over at Chris, then turned to me. "You okay?"

I flexed my hand and moved my fingers. I'd definitely fucked up my right. *Fuck.* I shook my head.

"Is it broken?" His eyes were wide. Fighters broke bones often enough during a fight, but going into a fight with a fracture was sheer stupidity.

But I needed this fight. And I needed to win this fight. So I was about to do something seriously stupid. "Let's re-tape it."

"Shit," Jonah said, giving me a knowing look.

He grabbed the tape, and we fixed up my hand as best we could. It still hurt like crazy, but I could deal with the pain. I just needed a whole new fight strategy.

"He'll expect you to come in fighting with your fists," Jonah said, apparently already on it. "So wear him out with kicks and your left. Make him dance around for a while. That way, when he pulls the fight to the mat, he'll be tired. Then use all that shit we've been working on for the last few weeks. Listen to me, I'll help you find your openings. He wants the fight to be about submission. Let's make it all about *his* submission."

I nodded and started visualizing the fight and the new strategy. It might work. It had to.

Determined, I pulled myself together. I could still win this thing. I started hopping again, the blood already rushing through my veins.

"Yeah," I yelled.

There was a knock on the door before it opened. A man with a headset and a clipboard came in. "It's time." He glanced down to where Chris lay on the floor. "What's wrong with him?"

Jonah shook his head. "He tried to force himself on a woman last night."

The guy smirked and toed Chris, who stirred a little. Then the guy said, "Must have been some woman."

Jonah laughed, but the guy was right. Kenzie was some woman.

Cade found us in the hallway and joined us as we headed to the arena entrance.

Forty-Six

The stadium seating was something to behold. Rows and rows of seats stacked up on one another that stretched up and back in all directions from the single cage in the center of the floor.

I followed Alexa down the aisle to our seats. I'd traded my VIP ticket in the second row with Cade so that I could sit with Alexa. It turned out that Cade didn't even need my ticket. He'd gotten a text from Ian asking him to stand in as a coach, so my ticket would go unused. But it was better this way. I could sit with Lexa, Ian wouldn't see me, and thus wouldn't get distracted.

Their tickets, however, were not as far away as she'd promised.

"How is fifteen rows back considered nosebleed?" I asked. We were barely outside the VIP seating.

"He won't be able to see you from here, you'll be fine." She waved me off. "Sit."

I sighed and obediently took my seat. It was good to have Alexa here. She might be annoyingly bossy, but at least I knew it was coming from a good place.

Although we'd only gotten there a few minutes before the fight was supposed to start, it still felt like hours until the lights finally dimmed and the stage lights came to life, dancing around the empty cage and over the full audience.

Music blared and the announcer began. "Ladies and gentlemen, our first fight of the night, Hayden 'The Gator' Jones versus Ian Leclaire."

Spotlights spun around the arena, and I cast my eyes over the audience. The place was packed.

I tried to imagine what it would be like for Ian when he came out after being introduced. Would he be nervous? Would he be excited to see so many people here? Would he even notice the people, or would he be so fixed on the fight that he had tunnel vision?

Gator was introduced first. He came down an aisle on the far side of the stadium, making his way toward the cage with his entourage.

As they approached the door of the cage, Ian was introduced. I searched for the spotlight that would follow him down to the cage, finally finding it just up the aisle from where we sat. Ian was in the spotlight, wearing his fight shorts, his gloves, and a look of determination. His muscles, normally bulging, were fully flexed. He was pumped up and ready to kick ass.

So effing hot. I regretted having passed up the chance to lick his eight-pack abs, and pushed away thoughts of their salty taste on my tongue as he walked within feet of me and I had to duck back behind Alexa. He continued toward the front, followed by Jonah and Cade.

"Where's Chris?" I asked.

Alexa shrugged.

I searched the VIP section and the people up front near the cage, but he wasn't there. *Crap.* This could not be good. Or could it?

Crap. I didn't know what it meant, but at least Ian was still fighting. I'd have to wait until later to find out what happened to Chris.

IAN

The stadium seating with the cage all lit up was just as insane as I'd imagined it. The crowd cheered as I came in, and I ate it up. I let each roar, hoot, and whistle inflate me and make me stronger as I made my way to the stage.

This was real. This was my day. Nothing could stop me. I thought you needed to take drugs to feel this high, but I was wrong. I'd made it here, to the place I was supposed to be. To the place I'd waited years for. It was finally my time.

On my way up to the cage, I searched for Kenzie. Knowing what had happened last night, I wanted to see her and make sure she was okay. Her seat was in the VIP section just feet from the cage, but it was empty. I tried to tell myself that she was okay. She wanted to leave, and Alexa would have gotten her on the plane safely. Hell, Alexa might have even gone with her back home since Cade had joined me up front.

Regardless, I'd already decided I would win this match for her. I'd promised her I would, and the anger I felt toward Chris would be enough to make it happen. Anger channeled correctly would help me pummel my opponent.

As I climbed up the few steps to the cage, the roar of the crowd and the heavy music followed. But when they closed the gate, the rest of the world faded away, and it was just me and my opponent. I was focused and I was ready.

Gator was a few inches shorter than me, which if I didn't know better, would have given me a false sense of security. But his shorter stature meant his muscles weighed more. He was stronger. This was also not his first big fight. His record was nine and three; he knew what he was doing.

I needed to be careful. All my moves had to be instant and deliberate. And he absolutely could not know that my right hand was totally fucked. He already knew about my shoulder injury; knowing about my injured fist would give him everything he needed to finish the fight in seconds.

The ref gave us his instructions, demanded a clean fight, and we touched gloves. Gator started off with his fists going at me. Which wasn't what I expected, but I was a boxer, so I easily avoided all his jabs. It was clear he'd spent a lot of time working on his footwork.

Still, his moves were practiced and I was a boxer first. I could anticipate every move before he made it. I ducked out, then faked with my right, jabbing him hard with my left.

My gaze fell on Kenzie's empty chair. She knew how much this fight meant to me.

Gator stumbled from my strike and shook it off. He came back at me. I blocked, then came back at him with more lefts. We only went on this way for a while before he started becoming weary of my left fist. He shook off my advances and landed a hit to my body. I fell back, and as he pursued me, I glanced at Kenzie's empty seat again.

She had to have stayed for the fight.

Maybe she was just running late.

MacKenzie

The minute Ian stepped into the cage, I knew something wasn't right. His stance was almost normal, but I would swear he was holding his right fist closer to his body, almost like he was guarding it.

"Does he look okay to you?" I asked Alexa.

"Yeah, why?"

"I'm not sure," I said.

"He looks like he's pumped and ready to kick some ass, if that's what you mean."

I shook my head and shrugged. "Maybe it's nothing."

When they started the first round, Ian and Gator exchanged punches, and everything seemed normal. Ian connected several times with Gator's face, and once in his gut. Meanwhile, Gator kept on missing his targets. It got to the point where he started backing up toward the wall of the cage. Gator was dazed and on the retreat. All Ian needed to do was give him one swift right, and he'd fall. But he wasn't using his right fist.

"I think there's something wrong with Ian's hand."

"How can you even tell from this far away?"

"I don't know. He just looks like he's hurt." My heart sank. If he was hurt this early, he might not be able to win.

"He looks fine," Alexa said. She nudged me and smiled.

I forced a smile and turned my attention back to the cage. Gator was coming out of his haze. He shocked Ian with a kick to the thigh, and Ian staggered.

"Shit." My hands went up over my mouth. "Come on," I whispered. "Please."

Ian swung around with his leg, aiming high, but Gator saw him coming, blocked him, and came back with a foot to his side.

My fists clenched. What the hell was going on? Ian was supposed to be the best on his feet, and Gator was taking him to school.

Ian was backed into a corner and took several hard hits to the face. He leaned in, grabbing Gator by the waist as if he was holding on for his life.

"Kenzie," Alexa shouted over the crowd's cheers. "You okay?"

I nodded and clenched my fists tighter, feeling like I was going to throw up. Ian had to win this fight; he just had to.

Forty-Seven

This wasn't how the fight was supposed to go.

Fuck. I held on to Gator, but he continued to jab me in the gut, so I pulled away and kicked his thigh.

Contact.

Fucking finally. He stumbled just enough to give me time to regain some ground, as well as my footing. I came back at him again, but he blocked with his arm. I was getting winded. I was also getting pissed at myself. I needed to turn things around if I was going to win this thing, but I couldn't find a fucking opening. I blocked more and more of his advances until the bell finally rang, signaling the end of the first round.

I went back into the corner, and the guys cleaned me up. I allowed myself to glance over at Kenzie's still empty seat. She had to have gone home. *Damn it.* I hoped she was okay.

The second round was more of the same. I made a few good hits, but he kept me on the run for a good bit. When the second round was over, I was starting to fucking hate myself.

I met Jonah and Cade, who brought water and helped wipe all the blood from my face. I was bleeding from a few different places.

Unable to stop myself, I glanced over to Kenzie's empty chair again.

Cade saw and followed my gaze. "She's up in my seat with Alexa. Row fifteen." He pointed over and up a little. I scanned the area he'd indicated until, at last, I found her. The arena was dark, but I could recognize her features in the soft light that touched the crowd from above.

She'd stayed to watch the fight after all. It was all the fuel I needed. Pride rushed through me, and adrenaline filled me.

I could almost hear her sassy pep talk. *You've worked too hard to start doubting yourself now. You're here because you're one of the best. Now start acting like it.*

I shook my head. I was supposed to be here. It was time to focus. It was time to finish this shit.

The bell rang and I came out swinging my left, then kicking. Gator blocked my fist, but I hit him on the side hard with my foot. I kept at him, throwing light jabs with my right, and following with quick lefts. He backed up into a corner and I held him there, punching and kicking.

The crowd roared, and for the first time that night, I knew they were cheering for me. It fueled me and I went at him harder, making contact several more times before he finally dodged his way out of the corner and grabbed me in an attempt to pull me down.

I held on to him, and he twisted and lifted. He wanted me down on the mat so he could get to work with his real skills. I was willing and ready, but made him work for it. He grunted and yelled, pushing past his threshold of strength, and kept fucking going. But my feet were square and I refused to budge.

"Make him your bitch," Jonah shouted from the corner.

And I did. Gator was pushing so hard against me that when I stopped resisting and twisted, he rolled over me, landing on his back. I jumped on top of him and started pounding his face. He tried to block me, but his face was red. Blood red.

He finally covered his face and managed to twist around, pulling up. We struggled on the canvas for several minutes. I couldn't get him in a good hold, and he was too busy on the defense to make any headway. But then he slipped out, landing on top of me, and grabbed my left arm and bent it back.

Fuck. He pulled and I scrambled, pushing myself up with my legs, trying anything to get out of his hold.

"You've got this!" Jonah shouted.

He was right. He'd shown me how to get out of this, but it was going to fucking hurt like hell. I bit down hard on my mouth guard, pushed up against him with my legs, swung around, then came at him full force with my right, connecting so hard the pain was unbelievable. It shocked through my entire body and I growled, thinking I might actually bite all the way through my mouth guard from the agony. My head was dizzy, spinning from the shock of my throbbing fist.

Gator let go of my arm and I spun around, wrapped my legs around his body, took his arm, and ripped it back.

He tapped out.

I let go and fell back.

Forty-Eight

IAN

"C'mon, Ian. You need to get that hand looked at," Cade nagged as we made our way back to the dressing room.

"Are you my mother now? I told you, I'm not going anywhere until I see MacKenzie." I held a bloody rag to my eyebrow with one hand and pulled up my phone messages with the other. I'd called and texted her, but she wasn't responding. "Cade, find out where she is."

"I'm sure she's fine. She's with Alexa. Your hand could be broken, we need to get that looked at."

I stopped in front of the dressing room and gave him a pointed look. I didn't have time for this shit. Kenzie had been through something horrible last night. She might have lied to me about it, she might not want me to know about it, but I did. And I wasn't going to rest until I saw her again and made damn sure that she would be okay.

Cade sighed and pulled out his phone, sending out a quick message.

We went inside, and I got cleaned up as well as I could with bottled water and rags, then changed into some clothes. I was still a sweaty mess when Cade heard back from Alexa that they were in their room, but since MacKenzie had been running away a lot lately, I wasn't going to waste time with a shower and a doctor visit.

MacKenzie

Alexa looked down at her phone again and typed in a message. I tried to get her to go meet up with Cade after the fight, but she'd insisted on following me back to their room, where we now sat on one of the beds.

"I told you, I'm fine," I said. "I don't need a babysitter. Go celebrate with the guys."

"Come with me," she said.

I shook my head. "Can't I just have some alone time?"

I was glad I'd gotten to see Ian's fight. I was through the roof about him winning. But I'd made my decision, I wasn't going to be a distraction for him anymore. And as proof that I'd made the right decision, he'd won his fight, all while thinking I'd already left town. How much more proof did I need that I was bad luck?

The door of the room clicked as someone unlocked it from the outside, and I looked over at Alexa.

She shrugged and got up, heading to the door. "Hi," I heard her say.

I assumed she was talking to Cade, though I couldn't see because the door was just out of sight. She went out into the hallway and the door shut behind her. They talked low just outside the room, then the lock clicked again and I heard the door open, then shut.

Silence.

"Alexa?" I called out, but there was no answer. I got up and headed to the door, but it wasn't Alexa who'd entered. "Ian," I said when I saw him.

He was bruised and cut up, his left eyebrow crusted with blood. His eye was well on its way to swelling shut, and his lip was swollen. Part of me wanted to reach out and touch him, but I didn't. He slowly made his way into the room, and I backed up until I couldn't back up any farther because there was a bed behind me.

I sat down. Why was he here? Had Alexa told him where I was? That traitor.

Ian took a seat on the bed across from me. I avoided his gaze as silence thickened the air between us.

Unable to take the silence anymore, I finally said, "Congratulations."

"Thanks," he said, but he wasn't smiling. He held his right hand up in the air, as if the simple act of resting it on his lap was painful.

"You hurt your hand." I resisted the temptation to go to him and check his hand for the break I was sure was there.

"Yeah, I broke it on Chris's face." His jaw clenched, and his eyes smoldered.

"You punched Chris? Why?" I asked.

"You know why." His voice was raspy, yet gentle.

God, I didn't want him to know what happened. Unconsciously, I balled up my fists, and when he saw what I was doing he moved forward, as if he was going to take my hands. I sat on them.

"How did you figure out what happened?"

His lips tugged up briefly in a proud smirk. "Did you see what you did to his face?"

I shook my head, then my vision blurred as I thought back to the night. "I didn't stick around to see what happened. I ran, just like you taught me." I wiped a tear from my face.

He crossed over to sit next to me, but I scooted away, making sure there was a safe distance between us.

His forehead creased. "Why didn't you tell me?"

"Because I knew you'd do something stupid." I sniffled and wiped at the tears again. "I thought you might go after Chris and get yourself hurt. I didn't want to ruin your fight."

I put my head in my hands. "And it turns out, you did something stupid anyway, and it did almost ruin your fight."

IAN

Kenzie could be so infuriating. "Don't worry about my fights, Kenzie. And don't you *ever* sacrifice yourself for them. Nothing is ever that important. Besides, it's my fight. If I want to do something stupid before it, I will."

Damn, I was still pumped up from the fight.

Her eyes widened and she blinked. Fuck, I'd scared her.

I took a breath and tried to calm down. "I don't understand why you think it's your responsibility to make sure I get to my fight. I've been working on this my whole life, and I'll keep on working on it. But there are some things that aren't worth it. The thought of Chris trying to force himself on you…" I shook my head and felt the rage course through my veins. "There are no words for how angry that made me. I couldn't punch him hard enough. I wanted to kill him. I almost did."

"Why? Nothing happened. He didn't…" She trailed off and hugged herself.

I put my hand on her back. "He tried. And I'm sorry. If I'd just fought harder for you, maybe you wouldn't have been there with him."

She shook her head. "I wouldn't have stayed with you. I couldn't. Chris would have pulled you from the fight."

I drove my right fist into the bed next to me without thinking. "Fuck," I yelled as shocks of pain spiked up my arm. I couldn't believe she really had stayed with him for the sake of my fight. "Why would you do that? It's not fucking worth it. This fight was not fucking worth it." I shook from the pain of my broken hand hitting the mattress.

"Ian," she said, leaning forward to take my injured fist in her delicate hands. "I did it because I knew you'd been waiting for this fight your whole life. I did it because I wanted this for you."

"But you kept all this from me," I insisted. If you had just trusted me, if you had just told me what he was up to, we would have been able to figure it out. *Together.*"

She bit her lip and looked at me, her eyes still glistening with tears.

I brushed a tear away from her cheek. "Kenzie, you don't have to do everything by yourself."

MacKenzie

"But I do," I said. "All my life, whenever I've needed something, I had to take care of it myself. Otherwise, it wouldn't happen. Besides, if I'd told you about Chris's plan to pull you from the fight, you wouldn't have let me do what needed to be done."

"You're right, I wouldn't have let you stay with him," Ian said. "Because it was the wrong thing to do."

"What do you mean, the wrong thing to do? I did it so you could fight. It was the right call." He was so infuriating. "I did it for you. But you know what, you don't have to worry about me doing things for you anymore. I'm over it. I'm moving on."

I stood up, and his arm gripped mine as I tried to pull away. He pulled me back down on the bed.

"Kenzie, wait, that's not what I mean. The reason I don't want you to do these things is that I care about you."

I balled up my fists again. "Ian, you have to stop pulling me close like this."

He moved closer and cupped my cheek, his eyes searching mine. "Why?"

"Because every time you do, it gets harder for me to pull away."

"So, it's true?"

I shook my head, not understanding what he was asking.

"Alexa, Cade, Jonah, and even Chris all think that you want to be with me. Do you?"

I shook my head. Not because I didn't want to be with him, but admitting it would be like admitting defeat. "I don't want to be a distraction. I don't want to be a burden."

"That is not what I asked. Kenzie, answer this. If I were someone else you couldn't distract, if I were a lawyer or an engineer, would you want to be with me?"

I looked at my hands in my lap and nodded.

"Then stop this bullshit."

I looked up at him, shocked at his tone.

His brow furrowed. "I've said it before. Being without you is the worst distraction ever. I almost lost the fight today when I didn't see you in the audience. I couldn't stop searching for you, I couldn't focus until I knew where you were and that you were okay."

He slid his hand around my neck and pulled our foreheads together. "If Cade hadn't told me where you were, if he hadn't pointed you out, I would have spent the entire fight looking for you."

I took a deep breath as I absorbed what he was telling me. Had he really spent the first half of the fight looking for me?

His voice softened. "I broke my hand on Chris's face. I did that for you. And if we'd been together, it never would have happened. Because when you're with me, I won't let anything happen to you." His thumb lightly brushed the back of my neck, sending waves of heat through me. "I'll never let anyone hurt you."

I made a small murmuring sound. His words were the ones I'd longed for my entire life. I'd always had to be strong, to weather every up and down alone, but by the solemn way Ian's eyes had latched onto mine and refused to let go, I knew he meant every word. He was here for the long haul, if I'd have him.

The thought was dizzying. I'd never had a forever person.

I could have just sat there looking into his eyes all night, but his lips were only inches from mine. With that realization, a need grew inside me. I had to taste him. I needed to kiss his lips and let him know that I was his. Slipping my arms around his neck, I closed the distance between us, gently kissing his bottom lip.

He grunted, and I pulled away.

"Did I hurt you?" I asked.

His mouth tugged up in a playful smirk. "Sweetheart, I hurt all over. But don't ever stop kissing me. It's worth the pain."

His swollen eye grabbed my attention again. I brushed it lightly and then kissed his eyebrow and his swollen cheek. I wanted to kiss away all the hurt.

I pulled away and took his injured hand. "Ian, we need to—"

He didn't let me finish, instead he pulled me into his arms and kissed me hard. I tasted metal and salt in his mouth; he tasted like a fighter. Brutal and powerful and strong. I wanted more. Even with his injured hand, he pulled me onto his lap so that I was straddling him.

"We need to take care of some unfinished business," he grunted as he pressed my center into him. He was already hard, and my body ached for his.

"Ian," I moaned. My body heated up, and I struggled to resist the urge to give in to him. I wanted this more than I wanted my next breath.

"Yes," he whispered as he trailed kisses down my neck.

"What about Cade and Alexa?" I asked, breathless.

"They knew I came here to make you mine. They won't be back for an hour."

With that information, my heart rate sped up. He was making me his in every sense of the word. It was everything I wanted.

"I…"

At a loss for words, I struggled to pull off my shirt, and Ian helped me as much as he could with one hand. Once the shirt was on the floor, his eyes drank in my bare skin with a hungry look.

"Kenzie," he growled, his gaze falling to my white lace bra. His eyes collided with mine, and seeing that I had no further protests, his fingers found the clasp and he unhooked it. He leaned back to look at me. "So fucking beautiful."

"Touch me," I whispered, and he palmed my breasts gently with both hands.

"Fuck," he said and jerked his right hand away.

I took his right hand gently in my own. "We need to get you to the doctor."

He wrapped his left hand around my waist and lifted me off his lap, placing me on my back on the bed. Then he planted himself between my legs and brushed his lips against one nipple, sucking on it. I arched my back, needing him to suck harder. He pulled away, teasing, his teeth gently grazing the peak.

"Please," I begged.

"You want to go to the doctor?" he asked.

"If you need to." I panted and pressed myself against him.

"Help me get my shirt off."

I did. His body was so amazing. I ran my hands over his chest, his abs, his back. God, he was so damn perfect. Every muscle in him was flexed, and his skin was so smooth. And his scent. I already knew I loved his scent, but after a fight, the flesh and sweat smell was all man. I wanted, no, *needed* him to take me right there.

Next I helped him out of his shorts. I thought I was prepared for the size of his cock, but as it sprang free of his boxers, I let out a little gasp and looked at him, my mouth hanging open. He was perfect. Huge and straight, and the tip glistening with moisture.

"Babe," he said in a low voice. "Don't look at me like that unless you want me to come right the fuck now."

His words were a command. I felt myself get wet, and my nipples, exposed to the air, hardened.

"What do you want?" I asked.

"Kenzie, I think you know what I want. I want you." He took his hard cock in one hand and started stroking it. "Are you ready?"

I was so wet, I needed him inside me. I nodded.

"Show me." He pulled me up on top of him and I straddled him. Grabbing his cock, he rubbed the tip over my wet opening and groaned. "Goddamn, you are perfect."

He held me by the waist and pulled me down on top of him as he pushed himself inside me, one slow inch at a time. "Tell me if this is too much. I can go slow, I can be whatever you need," he whispered, his eyes on mine and his cock pushing inside me.

My heart jumped into my throat and I felt filled with so much emotion, I almost couldn't hold it all in.

"More, Ian. I want everything."

My heart was wide open, and I was choosing to be in the moment and accept all the love I could feel radiating from his every touch. It was terrifying, yet amazing at the same time.

He pressed forward, his eyes never straying from mine as he filled me. I felt him deep inside me, filling every empty place so completely.

I gasped at the sensations and pushed my hands against his hard abs, lifting and lowering myself over him.

"Fuck, you feel incredible," he said on a groan.

I sank all the way down until I felt him in a place I'd never felt anyone, and then clenched around him.

"Easy, baby. You'll finish me." He held us there unmoving for a moment, giving me time to acclimate to his size as he got himself under control. "Now, go slow."

I eased up and back down, slowly at first, but the urgency quickly built. I needed it harder and faster, and it was all so good. I cried out as I let go. Ian gripped my thighs and pumped harder, and I felt him swell inside me.

"Ian…" I moaned, my inner walls trembling. I was getting close and wouldn't be able to hold out much longer, even though I never wanted this to end. Leaning down over him, I lowered my mouth to his. Ian claimed my mouth in a hungry kiss, his tongue dancing with mine in a deep, intimate way.

"Come for me, angel. I want to feel you let go." Ian's left hand moved to my hip and he pushed his hips up, meeting my pace thrust for thrust until we were moving in tandem as if we'd spent a lifetime doing this together.

I closed my eyes and blocked out all the years of little voices in my head telling me that I was unlovable and not worthy of someone sticking around. I rode him hard and wild, finally feeling free, until I came with a shout, repeating his name over and over again.

When I finally came down from my lust-filled haze, Ian was watching me with a small smile on his face. "Damn, that was sexy."

I picked up my rhythm again, wanting to make him lose all control like I had just done. It didn't take long. Using my inner muscles, I squeezed him again, and he sucked in a breath and held it.

"Fuck," he roared.

Seconds later, his cock jerked inside me and he grunted my name. His release was long and hard, and he held on to me the entire time.

As our breathing calmed down, he pulled me down to lie next to him, and he looked longingly into my eyes, not saying a word.

I met his loving gaze, and knew this was where I belonged. Why had I spent so long trying to stay away from something so right?

The answer hit me suddenly and made me sad. I wasn't used to people wanting me, and wanting to do things for me.

My vision blurred. I was tearing up, and for the first time in a long time, I didn't ball up my fists. I let the tears spill.

Ian pulled me to his chest and held me. "What's wrong?" he asked, fear and concern clouding his features.

I shook my head. "I just don't think I've ever been wanted like this before."

"I don't just want you, Kenzie. I love you."

Nodding, I wiped the tears from my face. "I love you," I whispered back, the words tasting foreign on my tongue, and yet so incredibly perfect.

Epilogue

IAN

Hearing those three words from Kenzie was like winning the championship in multiple weight classes. It felt fucking incredible, and even more so because I had to work for her love. Despite her tough exterior, Kenzie was still just a scared little girl, afraid to get too attached to anyone who might up and leave her. I hated that part of her past, but I vowed that I would make her feel loved every single day going forward.

I couldn't wait to get her home because that was where she belonged. With me.

"Ian, I told you, I don't need to live here," she sang as she followed me into my condo.

"It's either here with me." I grabbed her around the waist and pulled her close, kissing her soft lips. "Or you can move into my sister's." I kissed her again. Sophia was home from treatment and back on track. *Thank God.*

Kenzie pulled away and looked at me sideways. "You don't get to decide everything for me. I'm still in charge of me."

There was defiance in her eyes. I loved this sassy side of her, always rising to challenge me. It made me want to take her over my knee and spank her bare ass, not that I ever would. She would always secretly be the one in charge. Always had been.

"Fine, I'll get you your own place," I grumbled. I wouldn't have her living in that rundown apartment she had now. It wasn't safe.

She shook her head. "Ian, I can't just let you put me up somewhere. I have to be self-sufficient. I need to find another job. I can take care of myself."

After Vegas, Kenzie and I severed ties with Chris, that douche-rocket. It was easy enough for me to move to another MMA gym a few miles away. I already knew a bunch of the guys who trained there. Jonah even followed. But Kenzie was out of a job and refused to let me help her.

"But you don't have to." I felt my jaw clench and lowered my voice. "We've been over this. If you want me to sleep at night, I need to know you're safe."

"Fine, I'll stay here with you at night, but I keep my place." She looked up at me with pouty eyes.

I chuckled. "Fine. Keep your apartment. But I've got half a dresser that's empty and waiting for your panties. And over half an empty closet screaming for your sexy dresses." I drew a line with my finger up her side, tracing the outer edge of her breast. It made her nipples perk up.

Her eyes locked on mine, her mouth in a playful smirk, and my dick instantly hardened.

"Ian. I—" She gasped as I pressed into her. Her eyes drifted closed and she curled into me. "I know this is important to you," she continued. "I want to be with you, but I need to take it slow. I need you to be patient. This is all very new to me. Feeling loved. Giving love so freely."

"I know, babe, and we'll go as slow as you need," I said. "Take as long as you want. I'm not going anywhere. Well, actually I am."

I picked her up, hiked up her dress, and wrapped her legs around my waist. She smiled at me.

Fuck, I loved her smile.

"I'm going to take you to bed," I said and carried her into my bedroom. This was where I'd wanted her all along. Not in the backseat of a car or on the floor of my gym, but right here with me. Where she belonged.

Her arms clung to my neck and she kissed me, moving her lips gently over mine. It had only been a few days since the fight and my face was still cut up and bruised, but I met her kisses with my own, opening her lips and brushing my tongue against hers.

Her breathing intensified, and she grappled with the hem of my T-shirt, tugging at it.

I reluctantly set her down on the bed and helped her take off my shirt. Her gaze moved over my body in a hungry way that I loved. She could devour me with just a look. She undid my pants, pulling them down, and looked up at me with questioning eyes.

"What?" I asked.

"I'd push you down on the bed at this point and jump you, but I don't want you to hurt your hand." She bit her lip and smiled innocently.

"Where do you want me?" I growled.

"Lie back on the bed, please."

I did as she asked and she followed me, crawling up the bed and taking me in her mouth. Her eyes locked on mine as she sucked and licked my cock, taking it in like a champ, stroking the base with her hands. I brushed her hair out of her face, and resisted the urge to tangle my fists up in her hair as she brought me close to the edge.

Goddamn, that felt good.

"Kenzie," I growled.

She pulled away.

"I have to take care of you, babe. I need you to come for me." I moved to undo her dress.

"Careful," she warned. "Your hand is still healing." She pulled my splinted hand away and unzipped her dress, slipping out of it, then joined me on the bed.

"Down," she said and pushed me back so I was lying down once again.

I chuckled and let her mount me. Her legs straddled me and her warm eyes locked on mine. I slipped my arm around her waist and positioned her over my throbbing cock, then brushed against her opening.

She gasped and arched her back. I loved watching her get off. Her eyes opened and locked back onto mine. "Ian," she gasped and leaned down, kissing me gently with soft lips. As she kissed me, she brushed her wet folds over my rock-hard cock, then eased herself down onto me.

"Kenzie," I moaned. I pushed up into her as she grabbed my body, pulling me deeper inside her. She was hot, wet, and tight. She moved slowly at first, but when she clenched her inner muscles, I almost came for her right then. "Easy," I reminded her.

She smiled coyly but slowed down enough for me to get my shit together, then worked faster. As she rode me, her beautiful tits bounced above me and I cupped them in my hands, pinching her nipples with my fingers. Her walls started to spasm almost immediately.

"Ian," she cried as she came. Her walls tightened around me as she pumped up and down. I met her thrusts, and seeing her come apart, I was so turned on that I came with her. We clung to each other as our heartbeats raced together.

When we came down, she lay down next to me, curling up next to me, and looked up at me with her beautiful sleepy eyes and smiled lazily.

"Move in with me." I couldn't help myself, prodding one last time, forgetting my promise to go slow with her.

She smiled and paused only for a moment. "Okay."

"Really?" I said. "You're not just saying that because I rocked your world in bed, are you?"

She chuckled and playfully punched my arm. "Is that a bad reason to want to move in with you?" She paused. "Ever since the night we met, I've known I wanted to be a part of your life. Even on the days it was torture to be near you in the gym, so close yet so far away from having you. The harder I fought against it, the stronger my need to be with you grew. I've come to realize there really is no fighting it. So yes, I want to move in with you. Because I'm done fighting this. I'm ready to admit to myself that wherever you are, that's home."

Kenzie was finally where she belonged, and I couldn't be any fucking happier. Even if I never got to fight another fight in my life.

Acknowledgments

I would like to thank the fans and readers of Hard to Love, one of my bestselling books of all time, for repeatedly asking for a follow-up. Without you, Reckless Love would not have been born. Watching Ian–that sweet, stubborn, alpha male–fight for his shot at love was too much fun for this novel not to exist. So, thank you.

My deep gratitude to Liz Hellebuyck for your help with this novel. I'm grateful for your eyes, ears and plotting expertise. Danielle Sanchez, thank you for being an amazing publicist, and continually striving for new ways to help me share my books with the world. Thanks to Diva and Andy for your expert insight into the world of MMA. Any inaccuracies in the story's portrayal of the sport are due to artistic license. Pam Berehulke of Bulletproof Editing, you are a wonder. Your skills are tremendous, and I learn more every time I work with you. Thank you for your guidance.

A hearty thank you to my agent Jane Dystel and foreign agent Lauren Abramo for your hard work in placing my books in bookstores around the world, and helping to guide my writing career with a steady hand and sound advice. Helen Williams of All Booked Out, my cover designer, you get and accept my level of crazy. Yay! I appreciate your attention to detail and creativity. To my readers, fans and followers. You make this all possible and I am so incredibly grateful to you.

To my husband, John, for always believing in me. You never waver. Never falter. And there is just something so incredibly comforting in that. Thank you for being my rock.

The Gentleman Mentor

COMING MAY 2015

Fit, masculine, educated male, late-20's.

Discreet and forthcoming.

Under my direction and guidance women learn seduction techniques, how to achieve climax with and without a partner, explore physical gratification, and more.

Dominant, but don't be scared, kitten, I'm not into pain.

Do not be misled. I am pure mischief. But I'm the best kind of trouble.

So, what do you say? Do you feel like being naughty?

If you're ready to reach new levels of pleasure, contact me at @thedominantgentleman Serious inquires only.

About the Author

Kendall Ryan is the New York Times and USA TODAY bestselling author of more than a dozen contemporary romance novels, including Hard to Love, Resisting Her, When I Break, and the Filthy Beautiful Lies series. She loves reading about tough, alpha heroes with a sweet side, and aims to capture that in her writing. She detests laundry, and enjoys coffee, cupcakes, and being outdoors playing with her two infant sons and darling husband.

Other Titles by Kendall Ryan

FILTHY
Beautiful Lies

A New York Times & USA Today bestseller

I have no idea why she auctioned off her virginity for a cool mil. Regardless, I'm now the proud new owner of a perfectly intact hymen. A lot of good that will do me. I have certain tastes, certain sexual proclivities. My cock is a bit more discriminatory than most. And training a virgin takes finesse and patience — both of which I lack.

Sophie Evans has been backed into a corner. With her sister's life hanging in the balance, the only choice is to claw her way out, even if that means selling her virginity to the highest bidder at an exclusive erotic club. When Colton Drake takes her home, she quickly learns nothing is as it seems with this beautiful and intense man. Being with him poses challenges she never expected, and pushes her to want things she never anticipated.

A sinfully seductive erotic romance where everything has a price and the cost of love is the highest of all from New York Times & USA Today bestselling author, Kendall Ryan.

Visit Kendall Ryan at:

Website: www.kendallryanbooks.com

Facebook: Kendall Ryan Books

Twitter: @kendallryan1

CPSIA information can be obtained
at www.ICGtesting.com
Printed in the USA
LVHW081542271019
635482LV00005B/27/P